ESCAPE FROM MARIANNA

BOBBI BOLAND WHITE

Inspired by the true story of my father and his best friend
Persia White

WingSpan Press

Printed in the United States of America

Published by WingSpan Press, Livermore, CA
www.wingspanpress.com

The WingSpan name, logo and colophon
are the trademarks of WingSpan Publishing.

First Edition 2010

Cover Photography by Cassie Humphrey
Cover design by Mecca White

Publisher's Cataloging-in-Publication Data

White, Bobbi Boland.
Escape from Marianna / Bobbi Boland White.
p. cm.
ISBN: 978-1-59594-379-8
1. Reformatories—Fiction. 2. Abused children—Fiction. 3.
Florida—Fiction.   I. Title.
PS3623.H57 E82 2010
813—dc22

2010926349

10 9 8 7 6 5 4 3 2 1

For you, Persia, and for the "real" PJ
whose honesty and courage
made this story possible.

CHAPTER I

"What happened?"

Patrik stood beside Murdok's desk. The match he was using had burned to its end. For an instant it flared — blue, like gaslight in the narrow room. And then it went out.

" ... George?"

"I don't know. Listen."

They listened.

"Someone's downstairs," George crossed to the door and opened it. But the corridor was black — like a wall.

"Power's off," slowly he reclosed the door. "Maybe it's Murdok, Patrik."

Sliding now, into that murky space between seconds, fear coming up like quicksand in the room. Because at first they had thought it was Benson who had caught them, seeing their light as he made his rounds. And maybe he had.

But a larger net than Benson's had dropped, dark car purring along, twisting down through the black hills, gloved hand on the steering wheel, shotgun on the seat beside him.

Patrik looked across the silence at his friend, "Take it easy, George."

But of course, he knew. People always know when their time is up. Sometimes fate is kind and they know fast, thrown roughly into the future which is a relief and a blessing whether they're prepared for it or not.

And sometimes they know slowly, and this is more painful. There is a creeping to this kind of knowing because they are in two worlds now, one foot in each. And they cannot run. And they think through a thickness.

"Patrik, ... behind you."

Patrik turned. High in the wall above Murdok's desk some

concrete blocks had been removed. A metal fan set in a rusty box-type container had been wedged into the opening. Now while they watched a light bounced, then bounced again, along the outside wall, the casing, the fan.

"It's a trap."

"It might not be a trap."

But it was.

Patrik crushed the match between his fingers and let it drop to the office floor. Outside, darkness returned. A sheriff's car pulled through the gate, moved onto the grass, and rolled to a stop. Nothing moved.

"Jesus," George said softly.

And Patrik's heartbeat slowed. And his eyes closed. And his spirit went in search of Murdok like a hawk.

This was the State of Florida, Department of Corrections, Juvenile Division, 1960. And the war was on.

"Next month, Patrik, you will be sixteen." Tight, thin lips. "You realize, of course, you won't be going home."

Smiling when he said it, smiling when he hit you — a tall, bloodless man, incredibly thin, sinewy, incredibly hard for so thin a man. He gave the beatings. Murdok. He gave them in the "ice house," a small concrete block building thirty yards behind the dining hall. Sometimes Benson delivered you to him, down the dank corridor, into the filthy torture chamber where he waited, a urine soaked mattress on the cot against the wall, a three-inch wide leather strap under the bloodied pillow. This is where daytime beatings were given, scheduled beatings, beatings with witnesses.

But at night there were no witnesses. And at night, pulled from your bed, alone with Murdok, it was the dungeon, a thick-walled, airless storage room, cold storage, — no reason given, no explanation, dragging you barefoot through the low doorway, his grip on your arm like iron, pushing you down the narrow stairs. He had a chair positioned at the end of the room facing you as you entered, a dull light coming from the single bulb above it, the stench of sweat and blood thick in the room, choking you, turning your stomach.

"Take off your clothes, Patrik," flat, colorless eyes, "those are the rules here." The smile then, slow and cruel. "Take all of them off. Let's have a look at you, Patrik."

Murdok always wore boots, high ones, the kind that state patrolmen wear. And heavy jackets, the long belted style, grey usually, with a grey shirt underneath.

"Where's your hood, Murdok?" Patrik had said, because he had watched an interview once, on the small black and white television set back in Miami, an interview with one of the men who pulled the switch up at Raiford, the state penitentiary. The man looked just like Murdok, same type, about the same age.

The interview showed where the man lived, showed how the black hood was hidden in the woods and how on the morning of an execution he would arrive at the spot, put on the hood, and then wait there on the lonely road for the truck that would drive him to the prison.

The man had kids, showed him standing on the front porch of his home, showed a swing set in the yard. He said he didn't believe in Capital Punishment himself. Said he did it for the money.

Murdok, however, enjoyed his work. He was in the preparation phase now, taking off the grey jacket, placing it on the back of the chair. "This is your last chance, Patrik," he was saying. He had a tie on. That's right, a tie — to beat people.

Patrik had written to his brother about Murdok when he had first arrived, told Nathan what was going on, asked for his help.

"Last chance for what?" But shaking slightly as he said it, unsure of just how far he could push this man. Murdok's shotgun lay on the floor beside his chair. Patrik glanced at it, looked up again.

"Go on." Murdok was smiling. "Try it."

"Someday I might." Saying this but glancing away now, waiting for the beating to begin, *wanting* it to begin, wanting to get it over with.

Because although Patrik could defy Murdok to a certain point, turning his back, removing only his nightshirt, tossing it onto the floor, raising his arms to brace himself against the basement wall, he couldn't avoid what was coming next — the "ceremony" of it, Murdok's ravings as he paced the room, working himself up, swearing and cursing, ritualizing the damn event, accusing Patrik of perversions so bizarre

3

that Patrik's mind would stagger under them, grow numb, could not compute, grateful when the lashes finally began … three … four … telling himself it was nothing, strings of obscenities, so what? … six … seven … closing his eyes … hot searing pain across his back, … twenty-nine … thirty … sliding slowly to his knees … skin peeling off ….

"I might have to kill him, George." They had gone outside to talk about it later that night, sitting together on the grass. "I'll never let him get away with that again."

"Maybe you should wait, see what Nathan can do." George had looked at him quietly, "It's a serious step to kill someone." He paused. "You'd lose Lorraine."

"I haven't got Lorraine." Patrik looked away.

For a moment they were still. George smiled slowly. "Hey Patrik, remember Lowe?"

Patrik glanced back. He waited. "Why?"

"Can't forget him, that's all — how he handles things."

And it was true. Once Lowe was in, he stayed — just sitting up there in the corner of your mind evaluating everything you did. Lowe was so many things to so many people, an objective description wasn't possible. To the cops he was a nightmare, a lunatic right out of biblical times, but worse because he was also a damn criminal, only about 17 when he began his career, tall, dark skin and eyes, wild and gentle in the same moment, the same look, walking right into any store he felt like walking into, long matted hair, preaching and thundering down the aisles, taking any damn thing he wanted off the shelves, walking with those long strides of his, broken sandals flapping, right out the door again.

Lowe would always share what he had stolen, sometimes giving it away as he was going down the street, just handing it to some little kid, or old person, as the shopkeeper stood on the sidewalk watching, or raising hell, or occasionally running after Lowe.

If Lowe were caught, and physically handled, he was a master at backing up just enough to slip out of your grip, and then asserting a sort of shock field around himself. Probably it was that booming voice of his, and being so thin beneath that long loose coat he always wore.

Sometimes he'd laugh if confronted — just look at you and laugh, genuinely laugh, no anger or hostility in it like you might expect, just genuinely laugh, and then go on and hand the item back to you, like a child.

Lowe was a thief, yes. But having a political explanation for his crimes set him apart, confused people.

Lowe didn't steal; he "redistributed." And he was so damn poor himself, so dazed and lost most of the time, believing in a God that even the churches had forgotten, believing in a justice that the cops couldn't find in their manuals anymore, touching a naivety in the meanest heart — walking alone down 7th Avenue, school children looking after him, following him, calling on God to send bread to his people, calling on God to send hope to his poor, looking for Jesus in the humble shops, looking for Him in the eyes of everyone he met, even the wealthy, even the detectives, even the lame, and the incoherent, and the blind, looking for Him in *your* eyes, making you feel your own heartbeat as he looked at you.

"You know what's the matter with Lowe?" They had been quiet for a long time, still sitting together on the grass, most of the complex bedded down.

Patrik turned, looking at his friend. "What's the matter with him?"

"He's preaching to the wrong age-group. They're too old. Or else they're little kids. What can little kids do?"

"Yeah, well, that's all he's got. Who else is left?"

"That's what I mean. We're here. Most of us are in places like this. Maybe he feels guilty when he looks around."

"He can't help it if no one will arrest him."

"Nobody understands him, though. Not like we do."

"The cops understand him," Patrik said softly, "some people understand him."

And, well, maybe they did. Maybe a few of them understood.

But Lowe was barely hanging on himself there, towards the end. "I don't know how to help them, Lord," he would pray, head down, pacing up and down 12th Avenue — 6 p.m., cold, dark on the street, people getting off the bus from work. "I don't know how much longer I can keep it up."

"Don't you know who I am?" he would say, stopping, trying to look in the eyes of the people who passed by, most of them just ignoring him, trying to avoid him, fearful of him probably, a few of them laughing.

Rain now. Rain on Miami's streets. Rain on the sidewalks. Rain on Lowe's skin ... his hair. "They don't want to see me, Lord," he would pray privately, turning away, looking out into the traffic, water running down his face. "They don't want to use the eyes you've given them."

But some of them saw him — women especially, pausing, taking a moment to acknowledge him, to acknowledge the pain in him as well as the beauty.

Because there was always the beauty; one didn't have to look at it to feel it there, stark and compelling no matter what he said, like a fallen angel doomed to destruction for some unknown sin and yet in spite of this, or maybe because of it, frighteningly authentic as he stood there in the rain, fearless of the thousand terrors that beset the average man, concerned with the BIG terror, consumed by it.

"George?" Some of the cabin lights were on now, down the long hill from where they sat. "We should stop Murdok. I'm going to stop him."

"How do you plan to do that?" George looked at him.

Patrik didn't answer.

"Lowe's not always right."

"No? What would he say about Cottage One?"

George was quiet. Cottage One, fenced and isolated at the far end of the complex was completely dark. The youngest kids at the camp slept there, white kids mostly, no more than ten, eleven. They were tough little kids, skinny, freckles on their arms, their legs. Murdok kept them separate from the rest, wouldn't let them talk to anyone, wouldn't let them associate.

He beat them, though. Wednesday evenings. Everyone knew that Wednesdays, six p.m., were set aside for Cottage One. And every Wednesday after supper Benson, who was in charge of camp security, a black man in his early fifties but tough and wiry in spite of his age, could be seen leading one of the little kids from Cottage One, up the long road past the other cabins to the ice house.

It was a sobering experience — watching this shit. The older children would come outside and stand around on the grass, trying to imagine what it would be like for this little kid. And they would remember how it felt when they were new, with Benson watching as Murdok tested the leather strap, shivering, taking off their clothes and knowing it was wrong, blaming themselves for allowing it but terrified of Murdok, convinced he would kill them if they disobeyed, if they called out, if they turned, tried to get up from the stinking mattress they were forced to lie upon, gripping the iron bars of the headboard as the strap whizzed over their heads then *struck*, its metal insert doubling the pain … *whap!* … *whap!* … *WHAP!* … *WHAP!* … ten … twenty … thirty … slipping in and out of consciousness, unable to scream, drenched in blood and urine when it was over, filled with shame, barely able to stand, the shredded fabric from their cotton shorts embedded into their raw flesh.

Or maybe the older children didn't think of this at all as they watched the kids from Cottage One. Maybe they didn't think of anything. Some people close down early in life. They're just too innocent. It's just too much for them.

"Anything from Nathan yet?" It had been early April, grey and windy. They were observing the few visitors who had come to the camp.

"Guess not."

"What if Murdok calls you again — to the rape room?" They had begun walking back to the cabin. "Maybe you should have a plan. I know I've got one."

"Yeah?" Patrik stopped walking. "What will you do?"

"Just take that bloody club away from him, grab his arm and force him to drop it."

In the dungeon — the cold box, (by some it was known as the rape room,) Murdok did not use the leather strap. He used a club made of dead tree branches — four or five branches of different lengths, some broken and sharp, tied tightly together but not cut clean, left rough with outgrowths that would rip, snag at the skin and tear it, so that there was

7

often dried blood on these outgrowths if he had used this particular club before.

To protect himself Murdok wore gloves, pulled gloves on just before he beat you. It was during these final moments that he began the talking, while your back was turned. He would start by mumbling ... pacing around, his voice becoming higher as the accusations began, higher and more frenzied, almost like a whine, almost like an animal in pain.

"I'll probably do the same," Patrik had said. "I'd like to find some way to get that shotgun, though. And lock him up in there before I go."

But although this last was true, the plan that Patrik had begun to formulate differed greatly from his friend's. He had decided to wait until Murdok approached him. He would face the wall like before; he would wait, listening to everything that Murdok said. He would raise his arms and press his forehead against them. And then, when Murdok was at the height of his frenzy, when he had come as close to Patrik as he dared, then, at exactly that moment, Patrik would kick — kick Murdok back hard, kick him so hard and so fast that he fell.

And then ... but the plan always stopped right there. Patrik had to stop it because, somehow, in every scene that he envisioned there was nothing left to do, once Murdok was down, but to get his gun and kill him.

So that it wasn't the plan itself, it was the gradual deterioration of the plan that stopped Patrik from completing it. It was the unraveling of his life, right there in that room. He could not survive such an action. He'd be a murderer. He'd die in the electric chair.

And Patrik would imagine a resurrected Murdok (he used to dream about this) standing in his hood on the highway's edge. As if he couldn't kill Murdok anyway, no matter what he did. As if he would have murdered him, and lost Lorraine, for nothing.

Because although it was true, as Patrik had reminded George, that he certainly didn't "have" her, somehow, incredibly, it was still possible to "lose Lorraine."

Patrik had been in love with Lorraine since he was six years old. That's how long he had admired her. He wasn't sure if she was beautiful but it didn't matter. She was beautiful to him.

Lorraine was ... well, she was gentle. She had one of those soft, raspy voices. Even her laughter was soft. And she was intelligent. She was the smartest person Patrik knew.

Lorraine had a cousin who lived in New York, had won a scholarship to the City University. "So we can do it too," Lorraine had said, years ago when they were young, going off to Catholic school each day, believing that the world was good.

Even later, much later when Patrik had dropped out of school, sitting up with Lorraine at night, reading her books. Even then, they had tried to believe. And they would imagine living together in New York, taking classes at the University, sleeping late on Saturdays, watching the snow.

"And we could just be friends like that, forever," Lorraine had said, to use her exact words, to picture her saying them, to remember how her skin felt.

Patrik would always associate the Lorraines of the world with Catholic school. She had a little button that she wore on her jacket. CATHOLIC SCHOOL STUDENTS HAVE "CLASS" it read. And it was true.

So when Patrik was transferred to public school, when he realized that he was now voluntarily attending an insane asylum, (there was really nothing else to call it,) and because this new experience soon provided him with one of the truly great cultural shocks of his life, Patrik did what any sensible person would do. He just stopped going.

Here's how it happened. In ninth grade, two languages were offered: French and Spanish. Patrik decided to take French because, well, to tell the truth, after eight years with the nuns, the teacher just enchanted him. She was small and delicate with a soft smile and generous, fascinating lips. Almost like a white Lorraine — a French Lorraine. He used to go to school just to look at her.

She wasn't up to it, though. She was often ill, and when she did show up she seemed so frail and weak the class would run all over her. He used to feel sorry for her, wish she would assert herself a little more.

Patrik would always be ashamed of how long it took him to realize that she was a heroine addict. At the time he didn't know anyone who took the drug on a regular basis. He had never observed it like this, day after day. It was impossible to watch her, though, once he did understand. A person couldn't learn in that environment, he told Lorraine. And so he quit.

Patrik never told his parents that he had dropped out of school. He did this out of respect for them. And since no one from the school district ever came by, or even sent a letter, it was over four months into ninth grade before they suspected, and over six before they confirmed, that something must indeed be wrong because Patrik, although he went off each day with the others, was the only one who never brought home a report card. They still didn't mention it though, a tremendous credit to their faith in him. They probably know I study with Lorraine, he reasoned. But it was more than that.

"He's doing his best, Mrs. Williams," his father had said, pointing to the stack of magazines that Patrik had hidden under his bed. They used to make little investigative trips around the house when the children were out. Patrik's parents were extremely cordial to each other and always used titles when discussing their children.

"The foundation has been laid," Mr. Williams had continued, "and the pillars of knowledge have been chosen well." If you think this an amazing assumption — that Patrik, in spite of rampant delinquency, was building pillars of knowledge under his bed with stolen issues of *Time,* and *Popular Mechanics,* read on.

Bartholomew Williams possessed, among other assets, the gift of eloquence. He preached EDUCATION, not education. EDUCATION was not opinion; it was not a meaningless go-round with semantics. EDUCATION was INFORMATION, billions and billions of bits and pieces of clear, precise, definitive knowledge. In other words, THE FACTS. Without THE FACTS survival was impossible. Also, one could never learn enough of them because new facts came to light each day. Also, new facts about old facts came to light. One must STAY ON TOP OF IT.

So important was "remaining current" to Bartholomew Williams, that to live in his household was to exist in a state of perpetual emergency. One must always be alert. One must never miss anything. There were little verses he would quote, bumbling around the house in his bathrobe, nodding his head in approval of any activity that even remotely related to LEARNING THE FACTS, including of course THE NEWS, both the World Coverage at 6 p.m., and the National Update at 11 p.m., both of which were so potentially life threatening that everyone who was still awake would have to stop whatever they were doing and sit down quietly on the living room floor both to WATCH and to ABSORB.

"AND THE TRUTH SHALL MAKE YOU FREE" had been applied to Math, to Spelling, and to the Weather Report.

The process of interpreting knowledge, however, was not encouraged. The brain would automatically sort out, file, and re-arrange when it became in danger of overload. One must NEVER meddle with this process. Assessments and judgments would come in time. When you were young, your job was to accumulate.

He would offer helpful hints though, pointing the way to a future in which all the facts would be used. "The educated man is the man of tolerance, the man of peace, the hope of the world," he would say, smiling, locking up for the night. "The educated man is the just man," he would say, "and the Lord will uplift him in all that he does."

"Well, no offence against your father, Patrik," Lowe had said, "but that's just bullshit, man." They had been walking together down 2nd Avenue. "What has education got to do with Truth? Truth is something that you carry in your soul. It's instinctive; no one needs to read about it in a book."

"Well, education can't hurt. How could being educated hurt?" This was last summer. Lowe was still sane in those days; people still respected him.

"It can distract you — that's how. You lose your strength. People get addicted to it, like they do with drugs — rot away in basements reading papers all night long, up in places like Chicago and Detroit."

They had reached some shade now, a favorite spot of Lowe's under the on-ramp to the new expressway. Lowe had made a little home for himself under there, had some clothes rolled up, some revolutionary pamphlets, a candle or two. They sat down.

"Look," Lowe had said, "There's not an educated person in the country, not one, who really gives one flying F about the poor. They just don't care. They're causing it."

"Some of them care. How are they causing it?"

"By blocking it out. You've seen how they live, walking around in their suits and ties, taking vacations. They know what's going on. Little kids are dying out here on the streets, don't have enough to eat, don't have a decent home, don't know where to turn for help. Cops don't know what to do with them. What should they do — throw them into institutions so they can get beaten up some more? Educated people don't love God. They're full of shit. What good does all their education do?"

"I guess you're right." There wasn't any way to argue with Lowe. The best you could do was simply be with him, witness with him.

Lowe had a brother who had been disfigured. "Car exploded on him," Lowe explained. No one saw his brother after that; no one knew where he lived. It's possible he was involved in a robbery or two. "Only job that lets him cover his face," was how Lowe put it.

Lowe had a sister too. She was younger and she was — well, she was slow. It was pitiful to see her. Somehow she had managed to complete eighth grade; school must have figured they could push her through, just give her a certificate and hopefully get rid of her.

She was so proud of that certificate. She used to take it all around with her when she applied for jobs. It was dirty now, and crumpled. But she still took it with her. As if the fast-food places don't need people who can count. As if eighth grade is some big deal.

All day she would wander the streets in her long dress and dirty tennis shoes with that damn certificate. Maybe she was looking for her brothers out there, couldn't understand where they had gone. Lowe never said anything when he saw her, never called to her. He wasn't ashamed of her. It just hurt him too much to see her like that.

It was at the end of summer that Lowe changed. September ... October ... hardly eating, sitting up in doorways all night long, standing around in the rain, walking down the middle of 1st Avenue waving his arms.

"Losing his damn mind is what he's doing," Nathan had said. "Cops will kill him if he keeps it up. Some damn body's going to kill him." The only reason Lowe had survived this long, in Nathan's opinion, was that no one had the slightest idea what he was talking about.

"Well, I understand him," Patrik had said. "He sure as hell makes sense to me."

Actually, that was a lie. But Patrik was *trying* to understand Lowe, searching him out, trying to convince him to come in off the streets.

"I know what I'm doing," Lowe had told him. They were sitting on a wall outside the liquor store on 54th Street, just off 22nd Avenue. "I'm bargaining for time. I'm the last one. That's why I have to stay visible."

"Bargaining with who?"

"Who do you think?" Lowe had turned his head, looking at Patrik. "Who do you think I'm bargaining with?"

Patrik had seen Lowe one more time after that, right before he had been busted. He had been walking home with Calvin, late at night, all kinds of stolen shit in their pockets. It had rained earlier and the air was clean. Lowe was standing out in the street, not preaching, just standing there in some water. Patrol car must have spotted him; officers were telling him to move on, get off the street or they'd take him in. Patrik and Calvin walked right up to him.

"Hey Lowe. What's happening here? Are you all right?"

It was the strangest thing, standing there with Lowe beside those cops. It was as if time stopped. It was like the end of the world — not a sound, no one on the street.

"I'm all right," Lowe said finally. "These are my friends." It wasn't the words — strange as they were, that shocked Patrik. It was the fact that Lowe was smiling as he said them, bending down and looking in at the officers. And it reminded Patrik that Lowe had used to smile a lot, laugh and joke around like everybody else, so that he couldn't help but wonder what was really going on with Lowe, where he had gone in a few short months — eyes unchanging as he spoke, deep black sockets, skin so tight that you could see his skeleton beneath, not terrifying the way a skeleton can be, just sad and ... final, like someone from a nation in famine, too weak to be a real threat, just standing there beside the patrol car and looking in at those officers almost as if he really did understand them, the way that Patrik would feel later when he stood alone in the living room on 56th Street, with all that stolen shit in his pockets, watching the show about the executioner.

* * *

Patrik and George had been admitted to the Florida Juvenile Corrections Facility on December 30, 1959. On January 25, 1960, Patrik had given his letter for Nathan to a trusted boy who was being released. Knowing he would be searched, the boy hid the letter well, giving Patrik the victory sign as he boarded the bus that would take him to town.

Six weeks later, in early March, Patrik had experienced his first and only session in the rape room with Murdok. For the rest of that month, and all through April, he received no mail at all. Finally, in May, a white couple visiting their nephew brought Nathan's return letter.

Patrik would never forget how profoundly Nathan's letter had effected him. Nathan was doing all that he could, of course. He had contacted several people in the state legislature; he had filed a formal complaint about Murdok. He had even written to the governor. It wasn't that.

It was Murdok's credentials that shocked Patrik. Murdok had never worn a black hood, or for that matter, a white one. Murdok had attended private school and graduated with university honors. As assistant chief administrator for this facility, he was responsible for implementing all new corrective procedures. Currently pursuing a doctorate, his "study group" in Cottage One had been approved.

Patrik told no one about this letter, not even George. Then, on June 8th, Murdok had called Patrik not to the dungeon but to his office.

"You didn't think you'd get away with this, did you?" On the desk before him was a manila envelope; some of its contents had been removed and Murdok was sorting through these papers as he spoke. "Your date of birth?"

Patrik didn't answer. His nine month sentence could be commuted at Murdok's discretion to six; this would put it at June 30th, three weeks from now. Or, by staying out of trouble for sixty days he could earn an early release himself, which was what he had been trying to do, in spite of how it looked. For a moment Patrik thought that Murdok was telling him to forget it — he would enforce the maximum sentence of nine months no matter what Patrik did, holding him until September 30th.

"Twenty-nine July, am I correct?"

"That's right." Patrik looked again at the envelope. In the upper left-hand corner, the return address had been stamped: Commonwealth of the State of Florida. Office of the Governor.

"Good." Murdok looked up at him — a look that Patrik would never forget. "I have a birthday present for you, Patrik." But it was difficult to hear what he was saying now because his eyes, riveting in their emptiness, no pupil at all or one so small it could not be found, were moving as he spoke, "Are you ready to go back to court?" It was as if Murdok were reading something in the air, "Recurrent incidents of homosexual assault…"

Patrik looked down, breaking the spell. His heart was racing. 'Help me, God,' he was thinking. 'Don't let me lose it. He *wants* me to lose it. He's worried. He's setting me up. '

" … the coercion of children," Murdok continued, "in the performance of immoral and unnatural acts."

Suddenly, it was silent. Patrik looked up. Murdok was smiling. "You see, these are *your* crimes now, Patrik — not mine." His eyes narrowed. "If I say so, *you* will be charged with them — no one else."

Murdok paused, "I'll give you time to think about this, Patrik." He gathered the papers and slid them back into the manila envelope. "In the meantime, we'll have to find a treatment center to accept you, won't we?"

His voice changed then. "Now hear my word. If you try to run before this matter is resolved, you will be killed." He swiveled his chair around so that he was facing the wall, his back to Patirk. "I'll kill you myself," he said quietly, "if you try to run."

"Patrik," George stood against door. "Someone's here."

Patrik looked up. He didn't move.

George watched the crack between the doorframe and the door. Noiselessly, he turned the lock. Whoever was approaching had a light with him; he stopped, putting it down.

Silence. The doorknob turned. For several seconds there was no sound — none, anywhere in the building. Finally, George took a breath.

"Okay, he's going."

"Benson?" Patrik crossed the room. George nodded.

"Let's go then, follow him. Open the door."

"He's got that light — remember?"

"Just open the door."

"Hell, no." George turned, leaning back against the door. "I'm not going to let you do it, Patrik."

"Do what?"

George was quiet. Patrik forced himself to slow down. He walked back around Murdok's desk. "Help me take the fan out, then. I'll see what's going on down there."

But he couldn't see much. From the back of the building the blackout covered the entire camp, except … what was that? A flicker of light across the long field to his west. There was a road there, a private road that snaked along the western edge of the property. And there were trees, great sprawling trees draped with moss, perfect for a vehicle to hide beneath.

"Well?" The fan lay beneath the opening; George stood beside it.

"Nothing so far." Patrik slid back down. It's quiet. I'm going to jump." He paused. "You'll follow?"

"Right." George wiped his face. "Be careful. Go."

Patrik reached for the ledge, pulling himself up and onto his elbows. He turned. "You coming?"

George nodded. He glanced in the direction of the office door. "Just go, Patrik!"

The opening into which Patrik climbed was approximately fourteen inches deep and twenty inches high. For a moment he crouched there, sideways, filling the space like a big cat. He searched the distance. The light he had seen was no longer visible. Perhaps it had been an animal, a reflection.

Patrik lowered himself down along the outside of the building. For several seconds he hung there, gripping the ledge. He tried to relax.

George stood against the inside wall. 'I'll give him a minute,' he was thinking, watching the door. 'One minute.'

But George never got that minute. Because it was then, right then, as George stood waiting for Patrik to jump, that the lock turned and the door to Murdok's office opened.

CHAPTER II

George slid down along the wall, inching his way towards the corner. He stopped, not daring to move farther.

He could see Benson clearly now, standing in the doorway, the dull yellow light from his lantern spreading a path into the room. He was just standing there motionless as the door creaked open, as though he had pushed it and turned to stone.

George held his breath. The corner, deeply shadowed, was only inches away. Benson entered the room. Carefully he put down the lantern. The corridor behind him, filled with a ghostly haze, was empty. Good. He was alone.

George watched. Benson had a flashlight but for some reason hadn't turned it on. Cautiously he took another step, his eyes moving slowly along the wall. George got ready for the blast of light. He was crouched low, one hand against the wall, the other flat on the floor. Should he spring now? No, not yet. But then suddenly, as Benson stepped closer extending his arm and aiming the flashlight directly into the darkness where George hid, everything changed.

Because it wasn't a flashlight. It was a gun. Benson had a gun on him.

Until that moment George had not intended to physically harm Benson. His main concern had been Patrik, covering for him, seeing that he got away. He couldn't care less about himself. They could keep him here forever. Not that he didn't hate the place. Of course he did. But unlike Patrik, George had nowhere else to go. He had been staying temporarily with his grandmother, living with his box of clothes on her porch. But chances were she had moved by now, or put up a gate locking him out.

His father had done that — moved away slowly, in increments. A white man from the islands, he had visited often when George was young. These neighborhoods are not your real home, he'd tell his mixed-race children, walking down the street with them. You are French — Creole, like your mother. Intelligence, he would tell them, does not adapt to ignorance.

But talk is cheap and he let them adapt. And then, eventually, he left them there.

With George's mother, however, it had been sudden. "Alabama!" he had said to her. "Why in the world would you want to go there?"

"Look, you've got to talk to Mama," he had told his sister, helping her with her boxes, carrying them down the steps, placing them on the curb. "Does she think you'll be welcome, up there in those hills? You're not really white, you know. You're almost white. You *look* white, but you're not white.

"Just say it," he had pleaded finally. "Say what it really is," standing there beside her with the apartment all cleaned out, nothing left but a few paper bags, some old books. "Is it money? Because hell, I can *get* money — do you understand?"

"It's not that." She had looked up at him. "We'll have a home in Alabama. It's safer there. And besides," she had looked down again, "you have your own future to think about."

"What future do I have?"

"You have a future," she was speaking softly. "You can draw, can't you?" She wouldn't look at him. "You draw really well. Like an artist. That's a future, isn't it?"

"If I was going to be an artist," he looked away, over her head, "I'd have some damn pictures. What kind of artist…"

But it was over now and he knew it. So that what he actually was doing was hurting her for no reason, which was the last thing in the world he wanted to do.

So he stopped. And then they just stood there, on the sidewalk, in the warm wind of Miami, as their childhood collapsed.

We're not prepared for it — that split second before the countdown begins. *Do you have any last words? Do we have any WHAT?*

We feel tricked, stung, It takes a staggering amount of truth to change the way that people live, so much truth it's just about impossible to get it out. Because, for example, you can't justify. You can't say, Well, Daddy left and he loved us.

And you can't conveniently forget things — like the empty blue cottage in the Grove. For almost a year they had watched that house, hoping that no one would buy it, planning how they would fix it up, repair the porch, prop up the fence and tighten the wire for the tall white dog with brown spots and wagging tail who would live in that yard and keep them safe.

"You're welcome to come with us," his sister was saying as they moved towards the car. "Why don't you come?"

But he couldn't. They knew that he couldn't. The new arrangement didn't include him.

"I'll be okay," he had told his mother, "and ... good luck," because they had always said that to each other, whenever they parted.

And George could remember being very small — only five or six, going along on his way to school ... holding her hand. She would make up excuses to walk with him, talking to him as they walked ... thin, gentle fingers smoothing his collar, fixing his hair ... right there beside him every day like that, past all the little trouble spots.

"Good luck," she would say, when it was finally safe, leaning down to give him a hug.

"Good luck, yourself," he would answer, because she always seemed so young and soft, standing there smiling at him with her almond eyes ... in her red bandanna. Making his eyes fill as he turned away and walked into the schoolyard in the bright air.

He had gone back up to the apartment after they had left and walked around the empty rooms for a while. And then he had just collected his things and moved on down the street to his grandmother's porch.

His grandmother lived upstairs in a narrow, two-story house with vines and bushes all around it. He bought some drawing paper and some charcoal. Because their hours conflicted, George spending so much time out on the streets and some nights never coming home at all, his grandmother didn't feed him. It didn't matter, though. He could always hustle up a meal. And the porch was fine. There was an old sofa out there he could sleep on, and he stashed his most important things beneath it. At least he had his privacy. At least he had a place to stay.

And he had respected this. He knew his grandmother didn't want him there, would be relieved to hear that Juvenile had picked him up. And when she didn't come to court, he understood. She was glad he was gone. She wanted her porch back.

"Take it easy, Benson. It's me — George."

Benson stepped back a pace, lowering the gun a few inches. "Where? Let me see you."

George moved carefully forward.

Benson lowered the gun further, then further still. He looked at George, then behind him. Cautiously, he looked around the room.

"What's that?"

George didn't answer.

Benson was moving towards the desk, circling, trying to see what lay behind it, the bulk of which protruded slightly, an odd shape behind Murdok's chair.

"Come out," he said to no one — to the fan.

And then, in an instant, he was down.

"Okay, don't move!" The gun skidded wildly across the floor. Benson was struggling. "Just don't make me hurt you, Benson. Just lay still, damn it!"

One of Benson's arms was under him and he was trying to free it. George had the other one by the wrist; he yanked it around, pinning it to Benson's back.

"I said," he was straddling Benson now. He maneuvered one knee into the small of Benson's back, leaning forward and pressing down. "... don't move!"

George tried to rest. Sweat poured down his face, rolling into his eyes, stinging them. "You could have killed me, Benson. Do you hear me?"

Benson, exhausted, lifted his head. George shoved it back down. He felt Benson's forehead hit the floor.

"All right," George lightened the pressure on Benson's back, aware suddenly of the immense silence around them. "It's over. Relax."

Benson didn't move.

George lowered his voice, trying to speak and listen at the same time. "Let me feel you relax, Benson."

It seemed to George that Benson did, in fact, relax a little. "Okay, that's good."

George shifted his weight. He looked towards the door.

"Nothing happened. Have you got that? No one was here. You fell." Gradually he released Benson. "All right?"

George stood. Benson's arm, the one that was folded across his back, slid down an inch or two. His elbow hit the floor.

George backed up. "Benson?"

But Benson didn't stir.

For a moment George stood in the doorway. Slowly he lifted the lantern, letting the light move over Benson's back, his hair. Then he turned, walked into the corridor, and closed the door behind him.

George walked onto the highway just as it began to rain. A fog had settled over the camp and for almost a minute he walked slow and ghostlike in the white air, not on the side of the highway but down the middle of it — as if it didn't matter where he walked, as if he were invisible.

Just then, a tractor-trailer roaring down the steep hill from Dothan rounded a curve and saw him. Cursing softly the driver slowed, swung wide, then slowed again.

The truck was forty yards ahead, waiting on the road's shoulder, before George realized that it had stopped for him. The driver, watching through the prison fence, had seen something — a flash of light? But George was jogging towards him now so he ignored it. 'Poor kid,' he thought, 'God knows what's going on in there.' And then for reasons that were all his own, he reached across the cab, unlocked the door, and let George come aboard.

Patrik moved around the side of the building. He had fallen hard ...

SLAM, like a brick. Unable to get up at first, knees like water, crouched there on the dark grass.

For a full minute he waited for George, getting shakily to his feet, leaning against the side of the building. Perhaps George had gone the other way, slipped by Benson and gone out the front. But then, where was he now? Why was everything so still?

Stepping out from the shadows, Patrik looked west. A mist had settled over the long field where earlier he had seen the light. Time to go.

Patrik walked steadily. He was stronger now, heading directly south, deep into the camp. Ahead, less than fifty yards away, the grey phantom of the cafeteria loomed up before him. He had been there many times, walked down the rows of metal drums that held the prison's garbage. Like Murdok, he had often thought, rotting on the inside where it doesn't show, maggots crawling in him.

Patrik moved into the yard, making his way across the shadows without a sound. He looked ahead. Crates of produce lined the outside kitchen wall. He slowed. Something was wrong. He stopped, listening. In the darkness before him, something had moved. He waited. And then, slowly, his blood froze. And Murdok stepped out in front of him.

The rush of adrenaline that Patrik felt, coming face to face with Murdok on the dark path behind the kitchen, did not occur at once. For an instant, so great was his shock, he could feel nothing.

And then it struck. And it was loud when it struck, roaring and surging along his blood, lifting him up and throwing him off the path, pounding with him through garbage and wood, pushing him as he ran, down with him onto the wet ground, sliding and crawling back against the side of the building, feeling his way along its edge.

And then, suddenly, he was himself again. He could think clearly. And he remembered the door.

The kitchen had a cellar, dirt walls and floor, a fetid crawl space barely five feet high. A steep incline covered by a trap door allowed access from the yard. A similar trap door, although inside, led to the kitchen.

Patrik lifted the door, slipped into the crawl space, and lowered it quietly over his head. For several moments he waited. And then he turned and began to feel his way deeper into the black hole.

By the time Patrik entered the kitchen, raising the trap door inch by inch, aware of the noise it was making, the undeniable anch … anch … anch … as the rusty hinges turned, by the time he had laid the door flat on its back, pulling himself up quickly through the beams of wood, Patrik realized without a doubt that Murdok knew exactly where he was.

Patrik looked around the room. He picked up a gallon can of kerosene stacked with some others against the wall and uncapped it. Then, tipping it slightly as he walked, he moved into the dining hall and stopped.

No sound from Murdok.

Patrik looked down the long room. To his left one window after another. The door. More windows. Should he chance it?

A dense fog was settling over the camp. If he could get past the windows, if no one from outside could see him, he could exit easily and head for the cabins, or beyond them to the dark south.

But Murdok was here. In the kitchen. Behind him.

Patrik moved quickly. He pulled off his shirt, poured kerosene on half of it, and reached for his matches. 'Jesus,' he was thinking, 'I hope I know what I'm doing. I hope I know how to do this.'

But he was holding back. Destruction by most species is progressive. We like to flirt around the edges for a while, like the cat with the cricket.

Or possibly it isn't that at all. It's simply that we understand all form is tenuous, holding on to its expression in a universe that can absorb it instantly, forever. It is a frightening sight to watch a structured thing dissolve, slide down away from us revealing nothing at its core. We feel we must consider this new emptiness, prepare for it, 'weigh it,' as we like to say.

So Patrik paused. But not for long. Because it was then, standing flat against the wall where the windows began as the first of the sheriff's cars approached, crunching up the gravel path from the office, it was then — with Murdok moving into the doorway behind him, no breath, no sound, his long form like the shadow of death itself, that Patrik knew what he was going to do. Not what he would *try* to do; Patrik knew what he *was going* to do.

And so he did it.

But fires can have a will of their own. Aha! The horrifying truth we don't admit — a beingness that's always there, upright intelligence needing only a path, a beam, a route. Shiva with the face of a rat, seeking and smelling, whipping around corners, leaping across space.

Or a fire can lay on the floor and lick, like a snake, crackling slowly into consciousness. In either case, there's no control. So when Patrik's fire suddenly stood, pushing Murdok back into the kitchen, surprising him, tasting his skin, blindly scavenging for more of him to feed upon, Patrik was already gone.

That was the first fire. It blew the roof off the kitchen, melted the windows and sprayed ash on the road. But there would be more fires, erupting noisily as he ran sliding and falling along the road, passing cabin ten, cabin eight, watching the children slowly emerge, moving dream-like through the orange smoke, gathering their few belongings, fading into the dark trees.

One sheriff's car, at least, had spotted him, tearing behind him, rocking and crazed as it bounced along. He zigzagged, ducked and tried to hide. But on it came like a living thing, in mad confusion as it sought its prey, tires spinning, sure that its victim could not be far, searching him out with its white eyes, in the popping cinders and the black weeds.

It was one of the children from Cottage One who would stop it for good, turn it around, end the chase — coming out of the darkness, leaping onto the hood, sliding across it.

"DON'T LOOK BACK!" he called to Patrik, rolling back against the windshield, blocking the driver's view.

"DON'T … LOOK … BACK," imprinting itself on Patrik's mind, sounding over and over as he ran.

But Patrik was already gone.

And the rain came down behind him like a drape.

CHAPTER III

Home for Patrik was Liberty City, 56th Street, a few houses from the corner of 22nd Avenue. He stood now behind the little rusty gate long ago broken and left ajar by the countless, never-ending comings and goings of the children of this house.

It was twenty-two hours since his escape. He had walked all night, following at first the narrow unmarked road that ran behind the little country town of Marianna. There were no streetlights on this road, just tall bushes on either side, and several times he stopped, and found a place to hide, and listened. He had heard sirens as he walked, winding down through the wooded hills, but then the silence would always return, heavy, foreboding.

It was several hours before dawn when the road ended. Instinctively, Patrik turned north. There it was — the highway. But then, in the distance, he had seen a light, a single light moving slowly down the long road from the prison. There was no sound, no siren, just the light — like a light on the gate at the end of the world, blinking ... red ... red ... red. And so he had continued east, dissolving into the land itself.

Dawn ... muddy trail ... access to a paved road ... motioned onto the back of a truck ... bumping along ... sky beginning to lighten ... thirty minutes ...sixty ... traffic ahead. Now a crossing ... tracks ... freight yard ahead ... jumping down ... walking ... boxcars ... flatbeds ... jogging towards them.

And then, at last, he was on his way. And a great open sky lay over him — hours and hours of this sky, thrown on his back, drenched in sunlight, going home ... going home.

Until it was dark, changing tracks, clacking along, slower and slower.

And Patrik stood. And his breath caught. And all Miami lay before him — like a jewel.

Patrik studied his house. To be honest, it wasn't much — pale green with darker shutters, a glow in the front room, a glow in the kitchen.

"But it has flowers," his mother had said, standing in the kitchen of the crowded apartment back on 2nd Avenue, breakfast sizzling on the stove. "And it has trees," referring no doubt to the great wild bush growing up from behind, bending over the cottage, embracing it, dropping soft white petals over the roof.

"But most importantly," she had continued, "it will be safe." Not knowing that all of the mothers were saying this, agreeing with the City Planners, thinking the move was their own decision.

Patrik pictured his family. Six months since he had seen them. Maybe they had forgotten him.

In the yard next door the dogs had awakened and begun to bark. But now recognizing him, they came to the fence wagging their tails. 'Maybe time passes in a different way for animals,' he was thinking. 'They remember me. There's nothing to explain to them.'

But it frightened Patrik as he stood there, the quiet, the stillness over everything. Because Liberty City was running on E. Like the hobbled cars on the side of the road, little was left to salvage, and nothing seemed worth the cost of repair. Time for the wrecker. The riot. The war. Time to get those damn kids off the streets!

"Yo, Patrik!"

Patrik was crossing the street, just up from the light on 22nd Avenue, when he heard his name. He had not gone into the cottage, planning to locate Nathan first — find out how much, if anything, the family knew. But he hadn't realized how late it was, and the market where Nathan worked was closed.

Patrik turned.

It was Calvin, running towards him. "Hey, what's happening, Brother?" Stopping, … that look that only a friend can give … "what's going on?"

Patrik was beyond the lights now, on the dark grass where the housing projects began. Calvin settled in beside him.

"So where are we going?" Calvin gave his friend a quick glance-over. "You want to go over to my place?" This was actually where Patrik had been headed so they just continued.

"Have you seen Lorraine yet?"

Patrik didn't answer. Calvin was aware, of course, that the situation could explode at any moment but until they were safely on his street there was nothing to do but keep moving.

"Not yet. Is she all right?"

"She's all right. Things have been quiet, you know, a little tense."

"What happened?" They were deep in the projects now, walking more slowly. It was very dark.

"It was Lowe. About a week ago. He went down hard, tried to pull off a robbery." Calvin was talking rapidly now, no inflection, looking down as he spoke, so that Patrik knew right away what was coming and tried to get ready for it — if, in fact, it is ever possible to get ready for this kind of thing.

"He had a 25 — started shooting with it, challenging the cops to kill him, telling them to just go on and do it, get it over with.

"So they did. They shot him right there on the street. He's dead, Patrik."

"Jesus." Patrik bowed his head, turning it slightly in the way that people have to deflect such information. But it didn't help. He felt weak.

They had stopped next to Calvin's steps and for a moment no one spoke. Patrik looked up. "Where did it happen?"

"Seventh Avenue, outside the furniture shop. Remember … "

Patrik nodded.

"Well, they were waiting for him when he came out. Cops were everywhere, both sides of the street. You know, I believe they were afraid of Lowe. Not physically. Some other way, some way they weren't prepared to deal with. You know what I mean?"

Again, Patrik nodded.

"He had the money in a paper bag, threw it down, started laughing

27

at them. 'I don't even want your money,' started saying shit like that. 'Do you think I want it? Do you think I like your world?'

"He had the gun in his hand, standing there with it. Cops must have thought he planned to put it to his head, or in his mouth, blow his brains out right in front of them.

"He might have done it, too. But his sister was there." Calvin paused. "I don't know where she came from, how she knew. But she was there.

"She was calling to him, trying to push her way past the police, begging them not to kill him like they killed his brother."

Patrik looked up.

"Yeah, that too. Happened about a month ago." Calvin tightened his jaw. He looked at Patrik. "So she'd lost a lot lately and you can see how ... " He turned away. "Somebody must have been holding her back, because she just gave up then, and sunk to the pavement. She let out this ... wail.

"I never heard nothing like it — ever. It was so high ... and clear. So feminine. Just like a bird. It had a little quiver in it. As if it was her soul that was crying out.

"Lowe was listening to it too. They had a light on him. It was bad, Patrik. He wasn't moving. Tears running down his face.

"One of the cops couldn't take it anymore — turned the light off. He knew, all of them knew, if they never knew until that moment how Lowe felt, they knew then — all those years of pain inside of him.

"Lowe just went crazy from it, Patrik. Started asking them to kill him, started firing everywhere at once, up in the air, taking out windows, started bending down ... holding his stomach.

"They had to end it. Too many people. And kids. Little kids shouldn't be subjected to that kind of shit." Calvin took a breath. He lowered his voice. "Your brother Jason was there, with Robin. Saw the whole thing."

Patrik looked at him.

"I'm sorry, man." Calvin sighed. "There wasn't time to move them, get them out of there."

They were quiet then, sitting together on Calvin's steps. It had begun to rain, a light rain. They hardly noticed.

"Patrik."

"Yeah."

But Calvin needed no response. He knew what Patrik was thinking, what memory had been stirred. "She doing all right ... that girl from the playground. She's doing good, Patrik."

Patrik didn't answer.

"Maybe we should let it go — what happened that night. We were kids. What could we do?"

"If she had been your sister, or mine, we would have done something."

"Yeah. You're right." Calvin turned and looked into the rain. "1 remember too, you know."

They had come upon it innocently, climbing through the fence into the yard behind the elementary school. Summer, almost ten p.m.

The girl was on a picnic table, stretched out there with her dress up. She was young, about thirteen, but older than they were themselves at that point.

It was an eerie sight in the moonlight there, in the open yard behind the school where they all had played. There were six, maybe seven, boys around her, taller, older than Patrik and Calvin. They were just looking at her. They must have been planning to rape her. But then, when the moment came they couldn't, couldn't bring themselves to do it. So when they noticed the younger boys it was a relief, a diversion, and they called them over and pushed them up beside her and asked them if they wanted to try it. As if it were a joke. As if it didn't matter to the girl.

But it did matter to her.

And Patrik could remember how she looked — stiff and rigid, her eyes wide open but glazed, not seeing them. She never spoke, never made a sound. She looked like nothing he had ever seen before, with little chill bumps all over her body, the millions of fine hairs that usually cover a person's skin — not only on their arms and legs but everywhere, even on their stomach, standing straight up as if electrified.

And Patrik could remember how he put his hand out and touched her to see if she were still alive.

Nothing else happened. And when, several minutes later, Patrik and

Calvin just turned and walked away, nobody stopped them. He could still see them though, that strange circle of young men. Now, almost three years later, he could still see them — standing around the girl who was so frozen up with fear he thought she might be dead, unable even to touch her, just standing there looking at her, not even able to jerk off.

"Cal?"

"Yeah."

"I have to go away. They're looking for me."

"Where would you go?"

"I don't know. Up north maybe. I need to see Lorraine," he glanced at her house, next to Calvin's but dark, closed up for the night. "I should have tried to keep in touch."

But Patrik was only half aware of what he was saying, getting up and walking with Calvin across the grass, under the trees, looking out into the rain on 62nd Street. He had the strangest sensation as they approached the street, watching the puddles where oil had spilled and mixed with water on the black pavement, reflecting the blues and greens from the neon lights across the street. He felt that he was standing in a graveyard, and that he was talking to Calvin from one of the graves.

"It's all this … death in Miami." They had reached the corner. "It's hard to see beyond it, Cal."

But he couldn't break it; he couldn't come back, couldn't get rid of the feeling that Calvin was dead, that all of them were dead.

The traffic signal had changed while he spoke, turning to amber … red … and the streets were mirroring crimson … purple along the moving metal and the chrome of passing cars — running now, beneath their tires and along the curb, running like blood across the pavement where so much real blood had run. And Patrik looked at Calvin's shoes and he saw it there. And he looked at the sleeves of Calvin's jacket and he saw it there too. And he turned away and he tried to think of something else. And he would not look for it in Calvin's eyes.

It was almost dawn when Patrik returned home. Nathan had come for him while he was still with Cal.

"Don't make much sense, you know," he had said quietly, "spending the night in the rain when you got a home."

That's just how Nathan was. Sane. A big bear of a man, almost twenty, he was — at least in Patrik's mind, unshakable.

"Has Juvenile been by?"

Nathan nodded, "We thought you might be dead. Children said a ghost of you came by, stood up at the gate."

Patrik smiled. "No, I'm all right."

"Well, that's good, then. That's good."

For a few minutes they walked in silence.

"It might be safer for the family if I don't go home, Nathan." Patrik began slowing down. They were approaching 56th Street and the familiar scent of jasmine hung in the air with a thickness that was tangible. "I could always stay with Calvin for a few days."

"No one will bother you. They're all asleep."

"What about Daddy?"

"He understands. Here, take my key."

Patrik looked at the key.

"Take it. Go on."

"Will I see you again?"

"I'll be around."

Patrik put the key in his pocket. The streetlight was out where they stood and the cottage less than a block away.

"Nathan?" But Nathan was busy — holding down that street, that neighborhood just like a rock.

And Patrik thought about Lowe. And he thought about Lowe's sister. And he thought about the cop who turned the spotlight off.

They're just people, Nathan would say. Nobody knows where the dragon is. Nobody's sure. So the cop fights injustice as he sees it. And the crook fights injustice as he sees it. But the truth is that no one is fighting injustice at all. They're only fighting each other.

CHAPTER IV

Patrik let himself in quietly. To his right, across the small square room in which he stood, the door to the children's room was closed. Well, he had made it. He was home.

Slowly he began to look around. It all seemed brighter, more colorful than he remembered it. Through the archway to the kitchen, behind the table on which his father's bible lay — open in the soft light beside his cup, the door to his father's room was closed. Patrik crossed to the archway and stood there for a moment, waiting.

"I'm working to save each one of you," his father would mumble, chanting around the yard at bedtime, sprinkling holy water under the windows, reciting his verses with such conviction that even the noisiest child heard, and settled down, and grabbed a rosary or a toy, pulling the covers over his head.

"The Obeah man is coming," he would whisper. "... Oh, Lord, don't let him take my child," referring to the mystical powers of the Caribbean shaman to exorcise evil from disobedient children, a terrifying thought because no one knew by what process this "evil" would be driven out.

But things had changed. The magic was gone.

And now it was the father who hid from the son.

"Hi, PJ."

Patrik turned. "Hey ... hi, Sweetheart." It was Violet; she was seven.

"Are you all right?"

"Of course," he took her in his arms for a hug. "Of course I'm all right."

"All of us grew; wait till you see," she was leading him back through the front room towards the room where his sisters slept. Jason, who was only five, slept with Daddy now, his clothes in Daddy's closet, his shoes under the sagging bed where he lay in misery night after night, afraid to move because if he did the newspaper under the sheets would crackle — ashamed because he thought the paper was for "accidents" which it was, but not for his.

Violet opened the bedroom door. This was the girls' room, pillows and comforters tumbled about, arms and legs sprawled everywhere.

Their mother used to check on them like this, peeking in each night before she went to bed, standing in the doorway for a moment or two, the light behind her. "Counting her chickens," Maria would whisper, and giggle into the pillow.

But Maria was gone now, a young mother herself at seventeen. He used to steal for her. He stole for all his sisters, bringing them expensive magazines so they could cut the pictures out for school, or simply put up on the bedroom wall with tape — to dream about.

He remembered one of their favorites. *Seventeen.* Just thinking about it, all the glossy smiling rich girls, made his heart ache. Seventeen — like Maria. Seventeen — like Lowe.

Patrik closed his eyes. And for a moment sorrow pressed so heavily on him he could not move.

He never heard the vehicle that turned the corner in from 22nd Avenue, purring slowly down the street, parking under some trees.

But Nathan did. "I wouldn't stay here if I were you," he said quietly, emerging from the shadows, holding the shotgun straight down against his leg, tapping against the glass until it lowered an inch or two to hear him.

"I should have shot him," he said to Patrik later, sitting on the step outside the cottage in the first pre-light of dawn. "I should have shot him whoever he was." And then he laughed.

And all the heaviness that morning had in mind, looming behind the two of them, sniffing around just like an injured monster on that little street, reared up, and back, and clawed the air. And then, as Nathan laughed again, dissolved.

It was 6:30 a.m. when Patrik left the cottage on his way to Lorraine's and the sky opened. It was a deluge, splashing furiously onto the pavement, warm and sweet on his skin, making him smile as he walked, making him feel like a kid again, raindrops rolling down his arms like little beads of light. He was in tune with everything, all Miami. And he was going to see his girl.

Patrik walked up to Lorraine's door. It was so still. He knocked.

"Who is it?"

"Patrik."

For a moment she was silent, letting this sink in. Then the interminable fumbling around — lock turning, chain coming off. Until she had finally cracked open the door and taken a peek. With Patrik unable to say a word, scores of boyish hopes set off just by the sight of her. And then he was in, finally, and she had closed the door behind him, and he stood there dripping all over her floor, his confidence completely shot, just looking at her in the dull light from the kitchen. And he truly felt that he had been away for years.

"Rain got me," he looked down trying to brush the rain from his face. Everything about her seemed more delicate, more fragile than it used to be, the bones in her hands, and fingers. She touched him.

He looked up, into her eyes. There was a sadness there, a softness he had never seen before.

"Wait here," she was saying. "I'll get you a towel."

She went to the closet then, and he was watching her movements, awkward somehow in the large loose sleeping coat she wore, "Here, I found one," turning, walking back to him.

"Great. Thanks," taking the towel ...

By now, of course, he knew. Any fool could see what had happened. But he was trying in his own way to handle it so he just said nothing, looking away and moving into the kitchen, busying himself with drying off. He had brought a package with him — a change of clothes, a little gift that he had saved for her. He put the package down.

"Is your mother home?"

"No, she's gone to work. No one's home." She whispered this so shyly that he glanced at her.

"Well, come on then. Everything's all right. Why don't you make us some tea, so we can talk." He had finished with the towel; he put it on the back of a chair. "I brought a present for you."

Lorrain lowered her eyes. She had made no move to come closer to him, still standing right where she had stood when she came back from the closet, exactly where he had noticed what was wrong. He walked over to her.

"All right then, tell you what. You sit down, and I'll make the tea." He took her hand. He was trying desperately to remember the last time they had been together. November. Late November. But nothing had happened. Or did it? November — and now it was June.

"It doesn't matter," he would tell her later. "Don't worry. I understand."

"I wanted to write to you about it," she tried, "but I didn't know how. You don't mind, do you?"

"Mind?" His brain felt thick.

"Lorraine," he paused, "look … of course I don't mind. I never expected you to stop living. Did I ever ask you to stop living? Did I?"

There was no way she could answer. It was cruel to expect her to answer. "We can be … friends, like you said. Forever. Isn't that what you said?"

She tried to move her head in a non-committal way.

Grief was beginning to seep in on him now. He felt it as a weakness in his bowels, his gut. He pushed back his chair and stood. For a moment he watched her. "It's just that," he took a breath, "I've been away for a long time, Lorraine. Do you follow me?"

He stopped talking and listened.

She was just sitting there looking down at her tea.

He lowered his voice. "Lorraine?"

She was very quiet.

He sat down again. He lifted her chin so he could look at her, "Don't you know that people can count?"

He waited.

"Yes, I know they can count."

"You do?"

She looked at him. There was the hint of a smile in her eyes.

It blinded him.

It was almost eight o'clock when Patrik left Lorraine's. His plan was to find Cal, borrow some cash, and leave town as soon as possible. The last thing he needed now was his family. But there she was — Robin.

"You followed me?"

Robin didn't answer. She was tall, almost his height. He studied her; she was wearing black jeans and a white shirt. She was also wearing his old black cap.

"How's Jason?" They had started walking, "Is he all right?"

"Of course he's all right. We're taking care of Jason just fine, me and Nathan. We can handle it, Patrik." She paused. "It's covered."

"It is, eh?"

"That's right."

"So I can relax?"

"Yep."

"And if someone needs money, you can get it?" They had slowed down. "Answer me." Patrik reached out and took her arm. They stopped.

"I know how to get money. It's easy."

"You've done it?" She didn't answer. "Have you?"

"Not as a girl."

"I see." Patrik took a breath. "As who then? As me?"

She hesitated, searching his eyes. "Maybe. Sometimes."

"My God, Robin, are you crazy? Don't you know you could be shot? Do you think people hesitate — say, wait, hold on, I think that might be just a girl?"

"Stop it, Patrik." She pulled away. "I know all that. I'm not a kid." She looked down. "Sometimes it's worth the risk, that's all, to get things done. To get respect."

"Tell me this, then." They had begun walking again. "Is it worth your life? Caught by the cops, splattered all over the street like one of those rag dolls you used to have? Because that's how it looks. Guts come sliding out like snakes — I've seen it. Eyes rolled back, clothes all full of blood and shit. You want to die like that? You want to die like … like …"

"I know," she turned away, "like Lowe."

Well, they had to re-establish after that. And it took awhile, walking slowly, not talking.

"I've got to check for George," he said finally. "Want to come?"

They decided that Robin should go up the steps first.

"He's there." She was out of breath.

Patrik looked towards the stairs. "Wait," she touched his arm. "Take this." It was a scrap of paper and some money. "You can go to Texas, to Melissa; that's her address."

Patrik looked down. Melissa was nineteen; she had left home years ago. He counted the money — thirty-five dollars. "How do you know I'm going somewhere?"

She was silent.

"Answer me."

"Because maybe you killed him … that man … at the place."

"Did someone tell you that I killed him?"

"No. I saw his letter — about where he wanted to send you."

Patrik was stunned. "Did Mama see it?"

"No. I burned it. I always burn his letters."

"Well, I didn't kill him." Patrik looked down. "Maybe I should have, but I didn't."

"Still, you should go, Patrik. It's safer. In case …"

"I know. You're right. Thanks for …"

But she was moving away now, backing up, waving, just slipping out of his life like that — Miami's own. Forever.

George was sitting on the side of his bed, tying his shoes. "Place burned down," he said casually. There was a newspaper on the porch floor. He glanced at it.

"Right," Patrik nodded somberly.

"Must have happened after we left," George reached under his bed and pulled out a faded duffle bag. Slowly, he stood. For a long moment he looked at Patrik. His eyes smiled. "You ready to ride?"

CHAPTER V

Patrik made a pillow with his jacket, wrapping it around his bag of clothes, and lay down on one of the benches. He could see George clearly, sitting on the floor across the room, leaning back against the wall, eyes closed.

Miami was fading fast from them now. They had left at noon, rolling up the white highway past the small motels, the blue waters of the bay, passing through Fort Lauderdale, West Palm. And the highway had stretched long and flat as the hours passed, and the bus had grown cold as evening fell along an empty coastline and a grey sea.

They had hardly talked. They had been aware, though, hour after hour, of their position on the map, of the prison settled in the dark hills to their west. Ten hours and still in Florida. Night. And the road was black.

Daytona. Bus pulling onto the shoulder, driver collecting his gear, opening the door. No one moving. Silence. New driver coming aboard, standing there for a moment, silhouetted, reviewing his passengers.

And the old fear coming up. They could have our descriptions. Darkness. Someone coughing up near the front.

All right. It's okay. Door closing. Pulling out. If we could just keep going, not get off. Straight on through to Atlanta. We could walk from Atlanta. We could walk from anywhere in Georgia. How far could it be to New York?

Midnight. City streets. Traffic signals.

"JACK … son … ville." Bumping over the curb. Lights on. Air brakes. "JACK … son … ville," turning the corner, "Last stop … everybody out."

"No sir. Nothing local until morning. That's right, six a.m. Folkston, Georgia. You can buy your tickets right over there. Beautiful little town — Folkston. You boys have relatives up there?"

Patrik stirred on the bench. What time was it? He looked for a clock. No clock. For a while he lay still. Two police officers had come into the room. They were talking to the clerk, leaning forward so that the handles of their guns poked out behind them. After a few minutes one of them leaned back slightly, looking over his shoulder the way cops always do when they're being observed. Patrik averted his gaze. Across the room a large woman with a sleeping child on her lap dozed peacefully. For a moment he watched them. The woman looked kind. He wished he too could sleep, like the child.

But he couldn't. The ceiling lights above him glared with a white light that was merciless. And it occurred to Patrik that this was how it was when first the earth was formed — an exploding galaxy of gas and fire spinning and burning its way through space. And nothing could live in this blinding light; nothing could rest. Until God saw, and He stretched out His hand to slow the earth, and to cool it. And God smiled and He said, Let this be my gift to them. Let there be Darkness.

The bus stop for Folkston, Georgia turned out to be a little country store settled back from the road on the northern edge of town, two red pumps in front. The yard was deserted, though. And the store was closed.

"Maybe it's Sunday." They were sitting under a tree. "Patrik, is it Sunday?"

"Saturday." Patrik was studying a map he had found tossed on the grass beside the road.

"Well, I don't like being so obvious." George stood. "Wouldn't we be less obvious if we were walking?"

Patrik looked around, observing that there was no one to be obvious to. "You want to start now?"

"Might as well. Nothing else to do."

Patrik put down the map. "Okay. We could walk. You sure about this?"

George took a deep breath. He looked towards the horizon and then back at Patrik. "Why not?"

So that's how the decision to walk — from Folkston, Georgia to

New York City, was made. Amazing. Because although just strolling along for hundreds of miles was certainly an unusual way to travel, and although it has always been a great way to see America, it was still amazing, even to them. I mean, we're talking about a *very* long walk.

But the truth is, at 7 a.m., almost anything seems possible. And it felt good to be starting out that way — walking along the quiet road, sun on their clothes, no hurry … hour after hour … putting in the miles! It felt great!

They walked all day … resting at noon … cool water from a public pump … tall grass and fields full of flowers, cars that looked like toys under so much sky, rows of trees that actually gave syrup into little cups. Who could have known, who could imagine a place like this — a place where Murdok could never be.

And so the second day of their journey softened and cooled, and a great crimson sky covered them. And they sat together on a grassy hill and counted their money.

They were more than fifty miles from the state line. They had made it. They were on their way.

They passed through the town of Waycross just as the lights were coming on. For supper they bought some meat-pies and two bottles of soda, sharing this feast in a little clearing at the edge of town. And then they stretched out on their backs and looked at the sky.

And after a while night curled about them. And they, turning onto their sides, curled also — like the night. On and off, dogs barked. On and off, voices were heard. Night deepened. And Georgia stretched her long and lovely, treacherous self before them in their dreams.

The first clue that something is radically wrong is usually that the scene itself, although completely familiar, has been altered, added to. For example, where did George get that cover?

The lighting is different too. And it's winter. How did it get to be winter?

But it doesn't matter because once we determine who our hooded visitor is, dragging his bloody secret through the woods, we're after him.

We come out on a narrow pitch-black road that cuts straight through the trees. Now there is no way in the world that a tractor-trailer could be on this road. Yet suddenly we sense one, on our right; it is … huge. We feel along it, moving towards the front, stopping at the driver's door and looking up into the cab.

He's there of course. Murdok. But he's dead. A skeleton. He has no eyes.

The only really frightening thing about this dream was the fresh stub of a cigarette that they found in the morning, at the edge of their campsite, between the trees.

They walked for three days before they were offered a ride — dark sky heavy with rain, white pick-up passing them, pulling onto the shoulder, reversing slowly. It might have worked out fine if he had just let them ride in the back. They might have gone home with him, put in a good day's work, slept in his barn. But he had to have them in the front with him, all three of them jammed up together in that little cab. And he had to keep turning and looking at them.

Damn — forget the ride! Ain't worth it. Couldn't even breathe in there. Better to be anonymous, have some space around you. Better to let the weather and the countryside absorb you.

So that's what they did.

There is an "easing-in" that occurs when a human or an animal begins to trust the land, a gradual embrace by the environment, protective changes in structure and in mood — the way the branch of wood on the desert floor lifts up to look exactly like a snake. This helps the snake, not the wood. Why does the wood do this?

So when rain threatened they got off the road, and when darkness fell no one could find them.

Georgia, remember, along Route #1, is entirely different from Florida along Route #1 — even today. There's just no reason to be out there on the road at night. Don't dream a trucker's going to stop for you. He won't, even if he could see you which he actually can't, it's so damn dark out there, not until he's right on top of you, bearing down with such a roar it scares the living shit from both of you.

The problem is, in most places you can't walk. Thick woods line the roads, leaning in on them, blocking out the sky. Deep hills that plunge straight down, narrow bridges desolate and silent over black ravines. You'd have to be out of your mind to be out there. In the middle of Georgia? Without a light? Must have just murdered someone.

They were several days north of Baxley now. It was cooler at night and they had used up all their money. They kept matches with them however, and they were usually able to get a fire going, roast some greens they found along the way, or onions, young corn growing up beside the road. They were always hungry of course, but they were doing the best they could.

Toombs County. Heat. Nothing but swampy land as far as they could see. No food. Mosquitoes. The journey was starting to eat at them now, gnaw at them, visibly change them. Fear was starting to creep around, crawling under their clothes at night, bubbling under the thick mud, fingering its way into their dreams.

" . . . George?"

"What? Damn, Patrik! What are you doing?"

"I couldn't see if that was you."

"Who else would it be? Go back to sleep."

"I thought you were dead. You looked ... dead."

"Well, stop looking at me. I don't look at you, do I?"

And then, after an hour or so, "George?"

"Now what?"

"Maybe you should have kept that gun."

"Benson's gun?" George turned on his side, leaning up on one elbow. Through the tangled undergrowth only the occasional croak of a bullfrog broke the silence. "You know how loud a gun is?"

Patrik didn't answer.

For a long second George watched his friend. "I don't think it's a good idea, Patrik. Not yet, anyway."

So they dropped the idea of eating frogs.

Mid-day. A rise in the land. Some children playing near the road. Asking the children for water, asking if their mother could spare some bread but terribly nervous about this, watching the children run inside.

And then the children coming back with a pitcher full of cool tea, and biscuits — on a plate! And then, as if this weren't enough, some cornbread wrapped in brown paper and handed to them shyly by a little girl, "for later."

It was overwhelming. It was the most important lesson they had learned so far: to ask. It was all right, in Georgia, to ask.

And sometimes there was nothing in the pot but beans. And sometimes they would go away ashamed.

But the children of Georgia were always the same — calm and kind, watching them curiously, delighting in the opportunity to be of help. They seemed so at home with themselves; it didn't matter what their color was. Somehow they had learned the trick of being still. They knew how to wait — just look into another person's eyes, and wait.

An animal can sometimes wait like this: a chance encounter, a look that makes you realize that you are just as strange and interesting to her as she could ever be to you. Reminding you that it's okay sometimes to let your mask slip down. It's hugely funny but it's still okay to get caught, to drop the separation thing, the 'I am an intelligent, capable being and you're not,' thing, which we all know is a joke anyway.

But only a child can go right to the mark — smiling slowly at you, recognizing who it is behind your eyes who thinks no one can see him anymore.

Like Violet, Patrik would think. Like little Jason. And George would look away, and he would wonder how his own family was doing. And he would hope that the people of Alabama were just like this, exactly like this — even better!

He would think about it later too, lying under the sky, trying to get comfortable on his bed of clothes, cramped in a hollow between two tree roots, surprised that he had begun to reconsider a place like Alabama, surprised to discover that so far, he actually couldn't complain about this country of his, this astounding place that had hung so long unknown to him, on a wall, on a map, in a schoolroom on 22nd Avenue.

So he talked to Patrik about it. And they agreed that although their luck so far had been extremely good, they sure as hell better not trust it.

Do not think for a moment that they did. The fact that Georgia had been kind to them did not exclude their understanding of the burden of this state. They felt it, all right. The size of it. The inexorable weight of it. The aching of their very bones felt it. The highway at mid-day was merciless. The sun dried them, scorched their skin, cracked and split their lips. And sometimes, as they walked, the heat would move against them like a wall and press them almost to suffocation, and some days there would be miles and miles of this heat.

Until the road before them shimmered like water, like a river that had a life of its own, endlessly going from nowhere to nowhere — a raft moving them through seas of light, the only solid thing left in their world.

It took Patrik and George ten days to walk through Georgia. There was only one city, where the border slants across the northern edge of the state. An open, quiet city. A city of bridges, and sky.

But then again, they had entered Augusta just as evening touched their eyes, emptying the traffic, spreading an eerie calm across the closing businesses, the humble homes — their backyards empty now, and still. So they watched Augusta carefully, pausing on the first of her four bridges, and then the second. And on the third bridge they rested, and considered things.

It seemed strange, very strange. The peacefulness. Could it be trusted? Could someone of color make a home in this city, be blessed with a job, friendships? They had heard of course the stories of terror, the lynchings, Klansmen on horses riding across the bloody South. But the past had no real meaning for them now. Their own reality was vastly different — new and open, undefined. And yet ... what was the message here?

It was dusk when George stirred. "It's going to rain," he said quietly. "We'd better go."

But the power of this land would stay with them, the secret they had learned these past few weeks that wasn't taught in any history book. The living soul of Georgia is an awesome thing. Perhaps it's better not to question it.

At least, that's how it seemed to them. So when they turned east that evening, moving past the fourth bridge and down a long grassy embankment to where some laborers were camped, they accepted humbly the food that was offered, and they watched the sky for warnings, and they said little.

They had moved back, away from the fire, to sleep. It was midnight when Patrik stirred. He saw that George was already up so he got up too, and collected his things. They thought that no one noticed as they headed off again. But they were wrong.

"Why did they go, Sam?" one of the children who was still awake said quietly. "Didn't they like us?" And an older man who was also awake turned first to the child and then towards the road where the boys had disappeared. "They didn't even see us," he said finally.

They would discuss this once again though, in the morning, sitting up against the wall of an abandoned station house, cozy and warm, watching the steady drip of water running off the roof in front of them.

"Did you tell them they could stay and work with us?" she would ask him.

"Of course I did. It wasn't that. It's something else that made them go."

"I hope they come back. They weren't no bother to us, Sam."

"I know. They might come back. It's hard to tell.

"Sometimes it's too late;" he would say, "We've got to give them up to God. He's all they got but He's enough. They don't need you or me."

But they did.

They camped in a deserted lumber yard that night, glad to be on their way again, safely sheltered as the rain began, knowing nothing of what lay ahead.

And miles away, across the wet leaves, their future slithered to meet them. Slowly she coiled around the hills and lifted up her head, and put it down again, and hid. They had been put to sleep all right.

CHAPTER VI

It rained all day. At first they kept off the road, climbing above it, moving farther and farther into the woods, hoping the higher ground would be drier. But there were hazards everywhere, deep mud, wiry tangled branches blocking their path, forcing detour after detour as the day progressed, and the sky darkened, and the wind grew cold.

So they went back down to the road again, no shelter in sight, walking single file against the rain, heads down, sprayed with floods of water and stinging gravel from truckers who clung to the shoulder's edge, windows fogged, unable to see them of if they did wondering what in hell they were doing out there in weather like this.

Until even the truckers got off the road. And after one long hill there was another. Mile after mile. Four hours on the road and not one dry place to sit down. No houses ... no people ... nothing. Aiken County.

The first town they came to consisted of three flat blocks, the one in the middle being the business district, the other two residential. But the houses had a closed look, two-story houses with slanted roofs, set back from the road in dark yards, homes for the wealthy out of an old movie. There were no people on the street — no cars, no one walking. And for the first time they were afraid to stop, to use an awning or enter any public place.

It might have been the rain, or the reflection of a brooding sky in the shop windows, but the town had a haunted look, and the few faces peering out at them were a ghostly grey. Probably just the weather up here, Patrik was thinking, people need more vitamins. Which were comforting thoughts actually, the alternative — scenes of slavery, bodies hanging from trees etc. — not the kind of thing it's wise to dwell upon while walking through a place like this.

But then, magically, at the edge of town just as the rain stopped, a white grocery store all by itself with the lights on and the door open.

"Let's ask for work." Patrik checked out his own appearance first, then George's. "Tell them we'll scrub out vegetable bins." He paused, trying to see through the open door. "For food. Even old food. Scraps."

"Old food? You want to work for old rotten food?"

"Is rotten what I said? Did you hear me say rotten?"

They had stopped walking. "Just go in, George. Act white."

He waited. "Rotten is not what I said."

So George went in.

It was the Cadillac. Why did Patrik even look at it? But he was nervous, felt conspicuous. It gave him something to do while George was in the store, walking down along the curb, stopping to admire it.

And, "damn!" he would tell George later, "the sheriff came from nowhere, drove right over the curb, had his door open, almost killed me with it."

"Who ya runnin from, boy? ... threw me up against the car and handcuffed me. You saw how big he was — what could I do?"

And that's exactly how it happened, with George just catching the end of it, Patrik having been yanked around by then, squashed up against the car with the full weight of the sheriff against him.

"Nice car, ain't it?" the sheriff was saying, although George couldn't hear this part, "I can arrest you right here, just for lookin at it. Know why? Because why was you lookin at it, if you don't plan to steal it?"

With George continuing calmly towards them, getting himself into that 'I'll do whatever I have to do' mode, until the sheriff turned suddenly and saw him.

George stopped. The sheriff moved into his path. "We would be obliged, Sir, if you would kindly step into our vehicle, as I see you were expecting to do."

George looked into the driver's seat, then back at the sheriff. "What's the charge?" He glanced at Patrik as if expecting him to run.

"The charge ... is being broke. The charge ... is having no I.D." He was approaching George now, looming larger and larger, right hand on his gun. "The charge ... is sucking up all this nice clean air out here."

The truth is, if George had known how to drive a car, had ever driven one even once, he might have been fast enough to get into that police car and take off with it. But that wasn't his style. He had more sense. I don't care how many movies a kid has seen, you have to admit a move like that would not be cool.

People like to talk shit, though.

"If you hadn't been cuffed, I'd have taken that car." They were in a large square holding cell with benches on three sides. "Sheriff could keep us here for months."

"Yeah, but he won't. Right, Reds?"

In the corner was a white man, about twenty-eight, holding his head in his hands — blood caked on it. "He might. He might do any damn thing. Hit me with a board. I'll get even. You'll see. I'll squeeze his neck until his eyes pop out. How'd you like to see that?"

They were released about 4 p.m., allowed to wash up and fill some empty soda bottles with water. They were told to keep walking and don't stop because if they did, he — the sheriff, would be patrolling the highway and rather than chain them up and put them to work, he would save his energy by blowing their brains out right from his car. But at least he returned their things to them, even the pocket knife that Patrik had taken from home, even the two carrots that George had stolen from the grocery store.

Always remember if you have to shoplift, carrots and potatoes are your best choice. Aside from their excellent nutritional value, they are easy to hide, hard to damage, untraceable, and altogether pleasant to carry around.

So they set off in a fairly positive frame of mind, the road leveling out, the countryside clean. And by 8 p.m. they were 6 miles out of town and a slate blue sky trailing long edges of sunset lay across the horizon to their west, while to the dark north the first long distance lights from convoys of trucks coming out of Columbia blinked on and off like planets from another galaxy.

Somehow they lost Route #1. There was only one place where this could have happened. As night settled, the road they were on branched to the left. But there were no signs, no route numbers on this road, so they stayed to the right, rounding a curve and heading straight for what they felt was surely the highway north. If they had sought some elevation, climbed one of the grassy slopes that rose between the two roads, they would have seen that the fork to the left widened, stretching straight to the black horizon with its barely visible flashes of light, while the road they had chosen narrowed, undulating around the hills and disappearing finally, like a snake into the dark unknown.

"This is #302." They were sitting down, looking at the map in almost complete darkness.

"Shit." George looked around. "What happened to #1?

"#302 is an alternate of #1. Same thing."

"Patrik, how could this be the same thing as #1, and not a single person on it. Not one truck. Not one car."

Patrik didn't answer.

"What was the other road?"

"#78." Patrik squinted down at the map. "Nothing much on #78 either." Slowly he folded the map and put it away. "This is the best road, George, only one more day to Columbia. In Columbia we pick up #1." He stood. "Let's keep going."

9:00 p.m. Very steep hill. Becoming thickly wooded. Road seemed to be shrinking, solid grey line down the middle, hardly able to discern it.

9:30 p.m. A single house, top of the hill, plowed land beside it, two cars in the driveway. "They're arguing in there. Hear 'em?"

"I hear them. Keep going; don't even talk, Patrik."

Top of the next hill, rounding a sharp bend, something to the right — a house. No, a church, a shabby frame church with a sign in front: Bible Meeting Wednesday 7 p.m.

"Is it Wednesday? There could be food in there. They always have food at those meetings."

"It would be in the house — see the house?" A tiny house with one dull light hid behind a grove of trees. "We need water more than food; look for a hose.

"Come on, George," Patrik turned, "will you forget the damn food?"

"We should have stayed by that church, slept there. What's safer than a church? I'll bet there was plenty of food in there."

They were back on the road, actually on it, because there was nowhere else to walk, no shoulder, just the road itself with woods on either side - no moon, no way to see what was inside those woods although if something was it probably wasn't human.

"We'll come to something. It'll clear out soon."

Normally they would have been asleep by now. Georgia's hills had offered a profusion of shelter, old barns and lean-to's, deserted cabins overgrown with brush. They had made a habit of stopping to inspect these places, some with a table left behind, a mattress in the corner, an old pot. And they would wonder if black people had lived there and if the *KKK* had burned them out. Or if they had been white and had gone willingly, abandoning a life of labor that could not support them anymore, moving south or north with their families, their few possessions, and their dreams.

"Patrik. We've been going downhill for a long time now and we can't see what's down there."

"You want to rest? We could sit down on the road here."

"We could lay down on it too. Just go to F-ing sleep, right on the F-ing road. If it is a road. Which I doubt."

"It's a highway, George. It's on the map."

"The map can't be wrong? We could be heading straight to hell, people with hoods on down there."

"Nobody's down there."

But they were walking more slowly now.

"So what do you want to do?" They had stopped. "You want to go back?"

George looked at Patrik. "I really feel that we'd be better off on #1. It's harder to die there. People notice. Bodies get found. That road the sheriff talked about — where he could just drive by and wipe us out, was this one."

So they walked all night, back to the church, back to the house with two cars in the driveway, back to the juncture where #78 split away from

#302. And they started out on #78, and sure enough, after awhile it turned into #1. And by 4 a.m. the sky had cleared and the night was a windy velvet black. Occasionally a car or truck would pass but the road was smooth and wide and the lights hardly touched them.

They must have walked over ten miles along that road, stopping only when morning came, feet swollen, knees aching, resting in some high weeds but getting right up again when they noticed the swelling seemed to increase. They did make one more stop, using Patrik's pocket knife to cut around the tops of their shoes, extending the flaps they had made in Georgia. As far as the blood went, they just ignored it. Their feet were fairly numb by now and it seemed more important to keep going.

It was not until the sun was high that they finally slept, crawling under some trees beside the road. It was probably the heat, as well as the exhaustion that made Patrik throw up, kneeling down in the tall grass with George beside him, heaving and heaving with nothing but his own saliva coming up — just convulsing like that and unable to stop as the fortunate public on their way to Columbia drove by in air-conditioned comfort, not even looking concerned. Not even looking.

A person knows instinctively when he is going back to jail. He just knows. Physically.

Back on the road. Lexington County.

"Hey, George. Look here, I need to lay down."

"We already laid down. It's too hot."

"I need shade."

"Not now. Cops are watching."

2 p.m. Heat visible, no breeze at all.

"What cops?"

"Lexington County."

For a few more minutes they walked in silence.

"How long?"

"Couple hours."

"Same ones? Same car?"

George nodded. "It's okay. Don't worry about it. Forget it."

They slept that night in the bushes behind a service station, George waking up about three a.m. as a spotlight moved across the trees above them, making his heart thump.

It was a white car, a Plymouth, no lights on top, just plain black letters on the side: POLICE. It stayed in the area for what seemed like fifteen or twenty minutes, slowly circling. And then it screeched, leaving the concrete and turning inland down a narrow road, spitting dust and dirt as it disappeared.

There was a payphone on the lot and for a long time George studied it. To reach his mother, he would first have to call his grandmother for the number. Would his grandmother accept a collect call? Probably not. Worse, she might tell the police where the call had come from, if the operator mentioned it, which they always do. Lorraine had a phone. She could get a message to Calvin or Nathan. But what would he tell her?

So George decided to wait. He had found some change in the phone and he felt more confident now that he had it.

It's tempting to look back and say that George should have asked for a ride that morning. He asked for coffee, approaching a trucker who pulled in at dawn. He offered to pay five cents for the coffee, accepting a Styrofoam cup filled to the top — creamer, sugar, the works! But coffee is one thing and a ride is another. The money didn't give him that much confidence. It was only fifteen cents.

And Patrik was sick — wouldn't cooperate worth shit, wouldn't even use the hose to wash his bloody shoes out, said he was "conserving energy," said what he needed was a bath, a real bath, something that could "soak the poison out," he told George, glaring at him, "from all those goddamn spiders crawl up under my skin at night."

Truth is, the coffee helped. At least it helped George. And so eventually they started off again. Measured from Miami, they were almost half way to New York. Maybe all they needed was food.

Patrik knew about the fifteen cents. But the way he saw it, Lorraine was trying to have her baby — of course they couldn't call her. What kind of insensitive losers would do a thing like that? If they needed food, they could steal it. He'd be happy to steal it, he told George. Just tell him when. He was ready.

Stopping first though, little weather-beaten store, fruit stand out in front. Asking for water, drinking it out of a tin cup, Patrik noticing that his hands were shaking as he held the cup, careful not to drink too much. George taking control, wandering around, picking out some bruised fruit.

They decided to rest there, up a rise of land behind the store, under some trees. And Patrik knelt down on one knee, half way up the little hill, and he threw up the water.

5 p.m. evening. "Patrik, wake up. Trouble."

Patrik opened his eyes.

George was looking down the hill in the direction of the fruit stand. "South Carolina State Police — two of them."

Patrik shifted himself up slightly so he could see. The police were out of their car, walking around. One of them stopped, looking up through the trees towards where they hid.

"No way he doesn't see us," George pushed himself back until he was parallel with Patrik. He lowered his voice. "How do you feel?"

"I'm all right. Not too bad."

George moved back farther, gathering himself into a crouch. "Let's go then. Can you make it? Let's disappear on them."

They walked for almost a mile, well behind the tree line, before they saw the roadside rest. They had passed a few of these in Georgia but they were usually small, just a few picnic tables. This one however was like a park — green grass, lots of drinking fountains, a restroom.

"What do you say — should we try them?" They were watching a family of six at one of the tables. Afro-Americans, middle class. Patrik nodded. To George's credit, he was still acting as though Patrik were somewhat functional. Which Patrik wasn't.

"Okay." George observed him. "I'll do the talking."

They came out of the trees.

"Slow is good. Like everything is normal. We're just enjoying the day. Right? "

"Right."

Of course they didn't have a prayer. One look at the reaction they were getting and they knew it.

So although George continued to play his part, Patrik who was never actually a participant but who thought he was, decided to abandon his role altogether and just become part of the audience.

Well, it was a scene to remember — George pacing around this group of people, circling them, explaining in a very serious, very somber tone that his friend over there had developed a fever while they were traveling and then, wouldn't you know it, their car broke down.

And the entire time that he is building this elaborate story he is not looking at anyone — he is looking at their food. And with his hair grown out and matted, and with his back hunched over, it occurred to Patrik that George resembled that character *Wolfman* a little bit, especially as he was now talking more rapidly than ever to one particular woman and not even noticing how horrified she was, casually picking through the garbage she had just thrown out, actually eating some of it right in front of her.

And he kept digging in it. He even pulled out a dirty napkin and wiped his face with it.

But as George would tell him later — so what? At least they had food now, plenty of food. And best of all, from where he stood, he could see the sign on the highway's edge: Columbia City Limit.

7 p.m. West Columbia. Twilight. They were sitting around some trash in an empty lot, trying to eat.

"They could have helped us, George. They could have fit us in that car."

"There were seven of them, Patrik. How could they fit us?"

"There were six."

George didn't answer. Out on the street a lone police car cruised slowly by, German shepherd in the back.

"For one thing," George was still eating, "they were city people; city people are always suspicious — black or not." He reached for more chicken bones. The police car had passed them. "Why don't you just drop it, Patrik?"

"Because I have a theory about them, that's why."

George glanced over at his friend. Patrik was so glazed and crazy looking, even more so since the park incident, that George was considering how to hide him.

"They'd turn us in, if they knew we were here. City people are like that." Patrik leaned forward, lowering his voice. "It's a mental illness. I read about it. Cities can change people, make them evil."

For a few seconds George eyed his friend.

"So?"

"So Columbia — right here — is a city."

"Patrik. Relax." George smiled. "Have some chicken."

8 p.m. Dusk. Together on a long bridge.

"Sorry about how I was acting earlier. Don't even listen to me, George, when I get like that."

"You acted all right. Forget it."

"I felt ... bad."

"I understand. You'll get through it."

George looked ahead. Cops again, slightly past the middle of the bridge. "You know," he glanced at Patrik, "we could stay here for awhile. Get jobs. Get cleaned up. Maybe call home."

"Fine with me."

They both could see what was going on. A car had been pulled over — cops walking around it, trunk open.

George continued, "Kitchen work is easy to find. How do you feel? Can you handle it?" But old man fear had found them now, climbing up there on their backs just like a king.

"Of course I can handle it. Stop the shit, George."

They were passing the police car, almost past it. One of the officers turned and looked at them indifferently.

"So ... we'll start tonight," George almost smiled, so huge was the relief he felt. "We'll start looking for some serious work tonight. Right?"

Patrik let out a long breath. "No problem at all — first place we see, first restaurant."

They slept in a park. They decided that since it was so late now, so dark and quiet in this part of town, most of the restaurants, if there were any restaurants, would probably be closed.

In the morning they left Columbia. They never did find any restaurants, just lonely streets, tall buildings with grey windows and houses with slanted roofs, houses with porches and nobody on them.

They might have found help in Columbia, if they could have seen her. But they were like the man who, hearing noises in the yard at night, puts on the light before he looks out the window. Of course he can't see anything. Of course he's a target.

But that's how fear works on a person, turns the focus inward, makes you aware of the emptiness inside of you, between your ribs. It moves around in there, beneath your skin, forces you to deal with hiding it, works on all the little things like the nerve endings in your eyelids, your lips. In fact, most of the time you're so damn preoccupied you have to stare at an object just to determine what it is. You think you have time — it's moving so slow. So you just fixate on it. Like the doe on the highway as the headlights approach.

CHAPTER VII

"Patrik. You know what I noticed?"

"What?" They were headed northeast out of Columbia, grey sky, traffic very light.

"There aren't any children. Where are the children?"

Patrik sighed. "How should I know? Maybe we missed them. Maybe they're in school. Why do you care, George?"

"Maybe they kill them."

Patrik looked down the lonely stretch of road - thick vegetation on either side, no sign of life.

"I know what you mean," he said finally. "No one to talk to up here."

For a few minutes they were silent. George wiped his forehead. "We're runnin down, Patrik."

"I know."

"How long do you think we've got?"

"We've got awhile."

They slept in a ditch. "Stomach's messed up," George had said when they lay down to rest about 5 p.m., "feels like a rock."

Next day, dawn. Camden County. Cloudy sky. Puss in their shoes — crusts of dried blood rubbed off too soon, the sores beneath them raw, unable to heal.

"I'm taking my damn shoes off, Patrik," George stopped. "I should throw the damn things away."

Starting off again. Barefoot on the cool road.

They walked for about three miles before they saw the first police of the day, white dot in the distance. They were approaching a small bridge. Beneath it the land sloped down to a rocky creek bed — pools of water, clean and deep. They sat down by the water and waited. They took a drink. They studied the rocks.

"You think there's anything to eat in there?"

"Must be."

They were both listening. Nothing yet. But they had played this game before. Finally, Patrik crept out from under the bridge. He looked up. There it was — a white sheriff's car parked on the side of the road, windows down.

He moved to get a better view. The officer that he could see, in the passenger seat, was leaning back reading a newspaper. He was wearing glasses — round ones, tinted yellow.

Quietly Patrik made his way back through the weeds to George. "They're here," he said.

But George was lying on his side, back turned, asleep.

For about an hour, Patrik sat next to George under the bridge. And he remembered how sick George had been the night before, in the ditch. And he wondered if he had been wrong to tell George that sometimes it was better not to eat at all, advising him to throw those greasy chicken bones away. "We could stop eating for weeks," he had said. "Nothing happens. Lots of people do it." And he wondered if it were possible to be dying of hunger and not even know it.

It was dark when George awoke. For a moment he let himself adjust.

"Patrik?"

"Right over here." Patrik was lying on his back. He raised his head. "How do you feel?"

George struggled to sit up. His clothes were soaked with sweat but he felt cool. "I don't know. Cops gone?"

"Long time." Patrik watched his friend for a few seconds. "You hungry?"

"Maybe. Why?"

"I got some bread for you. Here ... catch it."

George caught the package. Two thick slices. "You met someone?"

Patrik lay back down, hands under his head. "Some girls. There's a private school up the road."

George strained to look at Patrik. He began to absorb what had happened. "Damn," he said quietly.

"Found something else too." Patrik sat up. "Might help your stomach." He paused. "It works like medicine."

George leaned back on one elbow. He looked at Patrik. "What is it?"

"Hold on," Patrik stood. "It's in the water. I'll get it."

For a few seconds George watched his friend. "How much?"

Patrik looked down. "Four bottles."

For a while neither of them moved, just looking at each other in the quiet dark.

"Don't worry," Patrik said softly, "nobody saw me."

And at the time, he had been sure of it. He had been confident that the owner of the sports car parked in the school driveway, with its top down and its back seat full of packages, would never miss the bag he had taken. OUR LADY OF MERCY Convent School, the sign had read.

And the gate was open.

He had gone around to the kitchen to ask for food when the girls had seen him, coming over excitedly, asking his name.

They had been so kind to him, inviting him to their graduation, telling him to bring his friend, describing the feast that was being prepared, the hundreds of families who planned to attend.

He was just caught up in it somehow. He thought it would be more appropriate if he and George brought a gift; he thought it would help them seem more respectable. But, to tell the truth, when he thought about it later, about George's condition that night and how insane it would have been to show up at that party, Patrik didn't know why in hell he took the whiskey.

But George understood. Or maybe he didn't care. They were destined to have their own celebration. They were destined to have their own "last supper."

So they washed off and they ate the bread, and they opened one bottle of whiskey and shared about half of it. They were saved.

They were redeemed. And for the first time in more than two weeks, nothing hurt.

"Patrik, I always meant to ask you. What do you make of it — this life we're going through?"

"Sometimes it's all right."

"You think it matters — what we do?"

"No. They tell us it does, but it doesn't."

George lay back. The sky was full of stars. "If there's a God, He should help us more. He should help the innocent people … little kids. Why should they suffer? Where is He for them?"

"It's messed up all right."

George rolled onto his side. For a moment he was still.

"Patrik. Do you think He got Lowe?"

Patrik looked over. "Yeah, He got him."

"I hope He got him before he was buried. I keep thinking about it, what it must be like down there. I just hope He got him before … you know, it rained."

For several minutes they lay quietly. Patrik closed his eyes. "Here's what I think. Maybe God was around once, but He left. He got busy with another galaxy where the people appreciated Him more. Every now and then He comes back. But it takes a lot. It takes someone He can call a friend, someone who trusts Him one hundred per cent. Like Lowe."

"I'm hip," George closed his eyes. "A friend is a serious thing — even for God."

What the subconscious picks up for future reference about most cataclysmic events is that you can hear them coming. A natural disaster hums in the air long before it actually strikes. An earthquake's roar begins with an audible vibration that builds slowly to the deafening crescendo that accompanies destruction.

Patrik and George were asleep when the police returned just before daybreak. They were asleep but they were listening — their bodies were listening.

So they did the right thing when the shouting began, the crashing of undergrowth, the kicks to the stomach. They moved defensively. They covered their heads. They rode it out.

If any of their possessions were recovered, they'd never know. The map was lost, the knife, the fifteen cents. They were beaten, handcuffed, dragged up to the road and taken in. There was no charge at first but later the police went back and searched the area, finding the whiskey.

You might recall that it was 1962 before the ruling that states must provide lawyers for the indigent at felony trials. This is relevant because Patrik and George were charged with stealing, a felony, and tried without counsel fourteen days later before a circuit court judge. Still fifteen but without proof, they were tried as adults.

"Maybe we should plead guilty, Patrik — ask for mercy."

They were on their way to see the judge, walking between two officers, heads down, unaccustomed to the outside light.

"You were asleep, George. Just keep out of it. You're not involved."

"Why am I here, then?" George glanced over at his friend. "If I'm not involved, why am I here?"

Patrik didn't answer.

George persisted. "What do you mean, keep out of it?"

Patrik looked up. It was mid-morning. They seemed to be walking away from the town, not towards it. Suspiciously he looked around. Nothing but grass, a few homes.

"Patrik, do you see this? Are you looking at *this?*" So authentic was George's reaction to the small white building to which they were now directly headed, that one of the officers turned and smiled.

"A church? Am I right?" George looked at the officer. "COURT is in a CHURCH?"

He was right. At the end of the road lay a long yard of green grass at the end of which the open doorway to a small white church was visible.

They could see into the church before they entered it. There was no vestibule, just an open room with a wide center aisle and folding chairs on either side. At the end of the aisle was a railing. Beyond the railing, back about twenty to twenty-four feet, more chairs, a semi-circle of them, some cops sitting there talking.

In the middle of the semi-circle, flanked by two tall potted plants, stood the lectern.

They entered the room and stopped. They were standing four abreast with the two officers at the back of the church. The judge, in flowing robes, was behind the lectern, perched on a swivel chair which had been swiveled up to an absurd height — an accommodation all the more bizarre because this was a man so diminutive in size, so shrunken and shriveled, he couldn't possibly see over that lectern. And so the only way he could address "the court" from that lectern would be to actually stand on the swivel chair.

Instead, he moved to the side. Patrik and George watched him. He peered at them from behind a plant.

"Look who they sent to marry us, Patrik."

They were led up the aisle and released. They waited. But, you see, it was over. The hearing had already taken place. Incredibly, they had missed it.

They never did have anything to say, standing there transfixed, trying to see what the judge was reading. "How old?" he was saying to the sheriff, looking up, squinting at them, "look like adults to me."

"No ... no," looking back at his papers, "never mind."

And then the reality of their situation was roaring at them. And the judge was gliding out from behind the lectern, robes billowing, his chair rolling crazily across the floor. He was headed right for them! Damn! Was he going to crash into them?

It was one of those experiences that the mind records in slow motion. It was just too fast, too bright, too mad to comprehend — this tiny figure rushing straight at them with his darting eyes, like an eagle on that flying chair of his, the folds of his robe draping his body, lifting and falling down again like the wings of some extinct predator. But where were his legs? Patrik and George stared as the folds of the judge's robe opened, closed, then opened again. No legs. Under the chair — nothing. No legs at all!

And BANG! He hit the railing with a jolt, turning the chair furiously around. Then again, faster, until it was spinning — actually spinning!

He was shrieking something at them now, still spinning, head thrown back, cackling and shrieking at them like a witch, like a damn witch! What was he saying? Years? Stopping then — full stop, right in front of them.

They watched his mouth. *"Six ... years."*

And then it came home. "Six ...YEARS." Yelling it at them. "SIX YEARS!" Actually screaming it at them!

They were numb, hurled backwards, unable to think. And the judge smiled smugly and with the fingers of his hands made a steeple, and he rested his chin on the tip of this steeple and he watched them until he grew bored. "Will someone come up here," he said finally, "and take these idiots away?"

CHAPTER VIII

For three days George didn't talk. He moved around; he managed. But that was the extent of it.

The judge of course had seen it all before — the traditional blank look on the prisoners' faces, circuits jammed. He knew these children were not idiots. But it's strange, isn't it? It's strange the way we count on someone who's been dealt a lousy hand to keep on playing anyway, to reinforce for all the rest of us the game he's going to lose.

"Hey, what's happening, Bro?" Patrik was trying to seem casual, leaning against the inside of the cage facing George's cot, which was over his. "It's not that bad. It's not the end of the damn world!"

George was lying on his back. He opened his eyes, glanced briefly at Patrik, and closed them again.

"We can appeal," Patrik sat down on his bunk. "They can't keep us here for six years — not going to happen — no way."

But he was talking to himself. So he stood again, crossed the cage and looked back at his friend. "What if I told you I have a plan? Something I'm working on. What about that?"

George sighed. He opened his eyes. "What makes you think I care, Patrik," he said finally.

Now the cage referred to was not a temporary cell. It was not a cell at all. It was a real cage, the kind that circus animals are kept in; this is exactly what it was but with the wheels removed, replaced by concrete blocks. Reserved for escape risks, the cage occupied center stage in a long room in which several dozen prisoners' cots lined the surrounding walls. Because cages like this had been used to transport slaves, and because this cage stood upon concrete blocks that were sunken almost completely below the floor line, it was assumed that the prison had been built around it.

The cage was in Bunkhouse One, for blacks, which was connected by an enclosed courtyard to Bunkhouse Two, for whites. The courtyard, accessible from both sides, was walled in front and back with eight feet of mortar and brick. It was, however, a sunny spot with showers, laundry tubs and clotheslines filling much of the space. Even the kitchen was in the courtyard, partially covered by a tin roof. Although the yard was shared, whites and blacks were kept apart.

An aerial view of the facility would show a simple "L" shaped structure set in a dirt yard surrounded by barbed wire, the long side of the "L" for the prisoners, the short side for administration. In practical terms this meant that the door to Bunkhouse One was always visible from the warden's office. The door to the white prisoners' quarters was also visible but farther away. The focus wasn't on it. At night, the light over the gate didn't quite reach it.

Patrik's plan was to escape through the courtyard, go over the wall and down along the back of Bunkhouse Two, and then go over (or under) the outside fence.

This plan ignored the fact that four strands of barbed wire topped the wall. It ignored the difficulty of getting out of the cage and into the courtyard. And finally, it ignored the fact that like every other prisoner there, Patrik and George were chained.

The less we have to say about these chains — leg irons on each ankle with a short chain connecting them, the better. Naturally they leave scars. They were worn not only when a prisoner was out of the complex, to prevent escape. Prisoners lived in them. They ate in them, slept in them, and bathed in them. Although the necks could be pulled up around the calves for some relief, they couldn't remain that way for long. Irons can actually scrape the skin raw, and if a prisoner is working in the rain or standing around in river water most of the day, naturally they're going to rust. According to camp gossip no one as young as Patrik or George had ever been seen in this camp. It was not a place for children.

'Something's got to happen,' Patrik was thinking. It was the fifth day. He was sitting on his cot listening to George thrash around above him. 'It stinks in here,' he thought to himself. 'No wonder George is crazy from it.'

And he looked at the yellow basin and the cracked toilet bowl at the end of the cage and he looked at the half empty bucket of water beside them, and he wondered if this was actually the plan — to keep them caged like this until they went insane from it, to never let them shower, or move around, or go to work like the other men.

So later that evening when Taylor — an old man, very thin and black, who was trustee for this bunkhouse, unlocked the cage to give them supper, Patrik took a chance. "Leave it open," he said, using his left hand to roll back the cage door as he took the plates. "Leave it like this. We won't go anywhere."

So Taylor did.

"How old are you, son?" he asked Patrik later, taking back the empty plates, rolling the door closed, locking it.

"Fifteen."

"You boys will be all right. Next week you work. When you work you can come out of the cage.

"Your friend," he said to Patrik. "will be better then."

But Taylor didn't know George.

Because when the first morning of the second week arrived and the long metal bar across the double doors to the bunkhouse was pulled, emitting a flood of light from the yard, George didn't stir.

"CAP'S HERE. UP … AND OUT!" A huge burley guard carrying a shotgun and two pairs of work shoes was heading straight towards them. He motioned for Taylor to unlock the cage, pulled it open and threw the shoes on the floor.

"The two of you," he looked at Patrik. "Move it."

Patrik picked up the shoes and looked back at George who was lying on his side, watching.

"Let's go, George." Patrik moved down the cage. He lowered his voice, "Come on, man."

George closed his eyes.

"He's sick," Patrik said.

The guard entered the cage, something that amazed Patrik as no one had done this, and walked up to George.

"You sick?"

George opened his eyes. "That's right." He looked at the guard. "I'm sick."

"You sick too?" The guard turned to Patrik.

"Yeah. I'm sick too."

Well, what could he do? Maybe George *was* sick. 'They might come back and beat him to death,' Patrik was thinking, 'if I leave him in here by himself.'

Good thinking. Not that the guards cared much, either way. In their eyes, two were just as easy to hurt as one. In fact, two were better — a bonus! A damn party!

Which was exactly how it went down — bunkhouse door pulled open, two men barreling in, two more behind them, yanking back the cage door, yelling and cussing.

Patrik luckily was on his feet, one arm up to protect his face. George, however, who had just managed to swing his legs down over the side of the cot, never made it that far. He was pulled savagely down to the floor, kicked, pulled up and thrown down again, then dragged out of the cage, across the room, and out the door.

It was normal procedure (minus the beating which was considered an initiation rite) for prisoners who claimed to be sick to be hung on the fence, handcuffed to it for the day. They would be offered a bottle of castor oil — medicine, to flush the bowels. If they drank it, it was assumed they had not been lying and the guards would go away and leave them alone. Patrik and George didn't know this however. So when the biggest guard, an over-weight, sweating, grinning horror with two teeth out in front, put the bottle of castor oil to Patrik's mouth, when he actually grabbed Patrik's face and tried to force the bottle between his lips, Patrik did what any normal fifteen-year-old would do. He kicked him in the balls.

The warden had to break it up — that's how bad it was. He had to stand on the step outside his office and fire off his pistol.

"You boys sick?" He was standing in front of them, cowboy style. The guards had gone inside.

George nodded.

"Castor oil cleans you out. If you won't take it, then you ain't sick." He paused for effect. "Got it?"

This time they both nodded.

"All right." He looked at Patrik and then at George. "This is a work camp." He eyed George down. "Means you work." And he strode off.

They hung there most of the day. About four p.m. the warden personally took them back to the cage. The next day they worked.

For Patrik it was a great relief to be able to work and he worked with a heart. To be able to exercise again, to be able to concentrate on something other than his sentence, was a blessing. If George had a problem with it — and he did, Patrik decided that he didn't care. He had his own sanity to save.

Usually they worked in a line, clearing off land, their long dull machetes swinging and chopping. But Patrik being young and strong sought out because he wanted to, because he was testing himself, the roughest ground — forging ahead through thick uneven patches of brush, dealing with stalks and roots, nests of small snakes and every variety of stinging insect, stopping only for water and again for lunch, driving himself as the day wore on through the heat and the moisture like a man possessed.

This was, to the other prisoners, an amazing thing. More amazing, however, was George's reaction to it. Because for every five feet … ten feet … twenty feet that Patrik moved ahead, George dropped back. And back. And back.

Sometimes he stopped working altogether, saying to Coats who was the captain of their work detail — a short solid Napoleon of a man accompanied on various days by guards from the camp who policed the line, tolerating this help but not needing it, commanding the team from wherever he stood in his long coat and his black hat just like Geronimo must have stood, still as stone on the hard ground, grey hair tied back, — saying to this man that he was just too tired, too sick to work, that he could not keep up this kind of work, that he was not cut out to do this kind of work.

Saying all this while Coats said nothing but simply watched him, evaluating him through slanted eyes, evaluating everyone through slanted eyes, eyelids puffed and swollen from lack of sleep because he never napped, never dozed, skin scorched and burned from years in the weather, the kind of skin that darkens red and stretches tight across the face and then cracks finally, exactly like dry land will crack. And if this kind of skin is not protected scales will form, crusting the skin on the backs of the hands, and even the fingernails change, thickening and turning yellow, curving inward as they grow, like claws.

Sometimes Coats would walk over to George, raising his shotgun, nudging him with it. George would go to the truck then and climb into the back. He'd lay there for the rest of the day, until dark, until it was time to return to the camp. And then Coats would go into the office to make his report.

And then George would be beaten.

Sometimes George would work the day, but he was always the slowest, the last in the line. "We have to get away from Coats," he said once, riding home at the end of the day. "You don't seem to see what we're up against, Patrik."

"I see it," Patrik had answered. "Just do your part."

"What happened to the plan?" George had asked him a few nights later, bumping along in the back of the truck.

"What plan? You know there's no plan."

"That's what I mean," George had said. "What's wrong with you, Patrik?"

This last statement seemed so bizarre to Patrik that he didn't even bother to figure it out. He didn't know what in hell to do about George.

But he was going to have to do something, because by the end of the second week George was being beaten every third night. And sometimes the sound of George's body thumping against the wall of the office would become so intolerable that the older prisoners, unable to rest, would start yelling at the guards to stop this shit before they killed the boy, raising so much hell that the guards would come into the bunkhouse to quiet them down, and usually they would bring George with them.

Patrik would not join in the commotion although he appreciated it, whatever the motives. He would turn his back when George returned, closing his eyes, pretending to sleep. And he would listen to how slowly George washed his wounds, how carefully he wrung the rag and let the water trickle over them.

What Patrik was feeling at times like these was a great mixture of shame and rage. George could easily do the work. Why was he forcing the issue? Had he been injured? Was something physically wrong with him?

Twice he had confronted George about this. But just as he had feared, George wasn't talking. "F you, Patrik," he had said simply.

And it got worse.

"So you like it here — is that it?" They were in the cage. The warden was working late that night so although George had spent most of the day in Coats' truck, he had not been beaten. (Beatings rarely took place with the warden present.) "You're enjoying this shit; it's fun for you. Am I right?"

Patrik didn't answer.

"Did you hear what I said?"

"I heard it." Patrik closed his eyes.

For a long time they were quiet.

"You know, you can be a cold son-of-a-bitch, Patrik. I'm not going to tell you one damn thing — know why? It's not worth it, that's why. It's just not worth it when you get like this."

Until the day finally came when George would not respond at all, even to Coats. They had been digging out a trench and Patrik had left his place in line and moved in beside George in an effort to help him, or shame him — he honestly didn't know which.

Coats had seen this and let it go. Everyone saw it. This was going to be the end of it, one way or the other. But it was going to be 'the other,' because almost immediately George moved to the side of the trench, jammed his shovel into the dirt and stood there, head down, leaning on it.

He would not go back to work. Neither Coats nor the guard Watkins who was with him that day — medium height, slight build but meaner than hell as if to make up for it, neither Coats nor Watkins could make him move. He wouldn't talk; he wouldn't look up when addressed.

"Let's go." Watkins raised his shotgun and aimed it at George. "To the truck. Move."

Coats, who had been watching from the rim of the trench, slid down a few feet and stopped, "Get away from him, Watkins." Watkins moved back, lowering the gun. "Go to the camp."

Coats moved into Watkins' space. He was concentrating on Patrik now, his shotgun raised slightly, the barrel pointing at Patrik's feet.

"Tell him to sit down."

"Sit down, George. Just do it, man. It's all right."

George sat down. He pulled the shovel out of the dirt and placed it across his knees.

And that's how he stayed, with Coats guarding him and the other men sitting down too, one by one, until the warden himself, led by Watkins, came rumbling and skidding across the mud and stopped at the trench with one more guard in the car beside him, the one whom Patrik had kicked in the balls.

What happened next would never have happened if Coats had stayed where he was. But Coats climbed out of the trench and walked away. He walked past the warden, got into his truck, and rolled a cigarette.

George, at that point, might have gotten up. But he never had the chance. Even Patrik who saw what was coming — saw the huge form of the warden's guard suddenly appear at the rim of the trench, even Patrik wasn't fast enough to stop it.

Because the guard leapt — threw himself at them, coming down so fast, with such a force, there wasn't anywhere to go. And BAM! his boot slammed into George's chest, knocking him backwards. Patrik threw himself against the guard, pushing him to the side, crashing down on top of him. For a moment, it was quiet. Patrik got to his feet.

The guard, panting, stood slowly, his massive frame unbending like an elephant seal emerging from slumber. Patrik moved between George and the guard. The guard was trembling now, red-faced and sweating. "MOVE," he raised his shotgun threateningly.

Patrik stayed. George, behind him, rolled slowly onto his side, reaching for the shovel.

The guard removed the safety on his gun. "You're going to move, damn it!"

"Okay, okay," Patrik raised his arms. He turned to the side, looking towards his own shovel. The guard swung around after him, giving George the opportunity to pull his shovel closer and use it to struggle to his feet. "Patrik," he said quietly, "look up."

The warden was standing at the top of the trench. He waited until the guard saw him. Put the F-ing gun down, he said with his eyes. Then he came down into the trench, sliding easily, walked up to George, pulled out his pistol and made his case. "Let's get you out of here," he said. "Come back with me. Come on."

"You too," he said to Patrik.

It should have ended right there. But the warden was overconfident; he put his pistol away when they got to his car, left Patrik and George standing there, and walked over to Coats who was by now sitting cross-legged on the roof of his truck — the only one with a commanding view of the whole scene.

Coats was facing them; the warden's back was to them. Watkins' back was partially turned; he was ladling out water to the other guard whose broad back was completely turned. Except for Coats, they were unobserved.

"I don't think Coats can see us."

"Yes he can; he's looking right at us."

But it was impossible to be sure. Coats sat with the sun directly behind him, his eyes narrowed to slits, his face shaded beneath the brim of his hat.

But that wasn't really it. What was so unnerving about Coats — what made it so difficult to know what he was looking at — was this: he had one glass eye. And this eye glinted at you when he turned your way, glinted almost diabolically.

But he was watching, all right, never moving as the scene before him crawled into motion, George stepping silently away from Patrik, raising his shovel (yes, he still had it with him) up and out into a backswing —

which made no sense to Patrik because the warden's keys were in his ignition, dangling there a few feet away, and once in the car it wouldn't matter who saw them, or even who shot at them. They'd be gone.

But George wasn't going for the warden's car. He was going for a different kind of escape.

It might have worked — this plan of his. But it didn't work because before his shovel ever made contact (he had hurled it towards the guard who had kicked him,) Patrik had sprung for Watkins, pulled him down and taken his gun. And through it all, he hung onto that gun, doing his best to keep Watkins down, shouting at George to go ... GO! ... just get in the F-ing car and GO!

No shots were fired. By the time the warden had turned around, George's shovel, retrieved by the guard whom it had barely grazed (but in whom had awakened so satanic a rage that George was temporarily paralyzed by it,) this shovel on its mission back to George could not be stopped.

Even the warden couldn't stop it. In a wild arc it struck Patrik first, (barely missing Watkins who fortunately for him was still under Patrik,) and then like a kite gone out of control it went straight for George, down and then up in a giant V, smashing his shoulder, cutting his face, and almost slicing off his ear.

The warden did glance back at Coats, right before he got into his car. But Coats hadn't moved, his face still shadowed, the sun behind him a bloody red.

It was dawn before Patrik could lift his head. Taylor came in with a fresh bucket of water, some clean rags, and some coffee, but when no one responded he left again.

Sometime around mid-morning George got up. He moved slowly to the toilet, used it, and poured some water into the sink. He came back and stopped by Patrik's cot. He crouched down, "Patrik, are you all right?"

"I'm all right."

"Sorry about what you did yesterday. 1 thought you'd take the car and go."

"Sure you did." Patrik moved painfully. He sat up on the edge of his cot, supporting his head with his hands. "Watkins would have shot you. Remember him?"

George didn't answer.

Patrik waited. He looked up. "What's wrong?"

"I need some help. Can you get up?" George moved to the end of the cage and stopped. "See the water?"

Patrik walked up to the sink. It was plugged with a piece of rag and it was filled to the top. "I see it."

George began speaking quietly now, very calmly, as he had not spoken in weeks. Everything about him seemed normal, everything except what he was saying. And what he was saying was so insane that it was almost unintelligible.

"1 want you to know that this is the best way, Patrik, at least for me. You're doing okay here, but I'm not."

"Hey, George, what are you saying? Come on, man." Patrik looked away, "stop this shit."

George had been leaning over the sink, head down. He straightened now and Patrik noticed how terribly swollen his face was and how his shoulder hung as if his collarbone had snapped. "You're my friend, Patrik," he was saying, " … just help me, okay?"

"Jesus," Patrik sighed, "I don't believe this."

"Will you help me or not?"

"Hell no. Nobody does it like this, George. Why don't you make Coats kill you. Or one of the guards."

George didn't answer.

"They'll charge me with it, say we argued."

George looked back at the water. "No they won't. They don't care." He looked up. "It's not your problem, Patrik."

But George had said this last so seriously, and he had stood there glaring at Patrik so intently above the little bowl of water, that suddenly — for no reason he could name, Patrik almost laughed.

"All right." Patrik stepped closer. "Okay — let's do it."

George bent over the sink, closing his eyes.

"Ready? Now!" Patrik pressed down hard on George's back, pushing his head under the water. "If this isn't stupid … "

Ten seconds … twenty … twenty-five. Patrik tightened his grip on George's hair. "Can't keep up the pace — why not? Rest of the team keeps up. They manage."

Thirty seconds. "You think it's easy for them? You think they like it? You think everyone is enjoying it out there?"

Patrik lightened the pressure. George had been under for 50 seconds. "All right, I get the point, George."

There was blood in the water from George's wounds. 'He won't die,' Patrik was thinking. 'If he passes out, I can always pump the water out of him.'

But George had heard him. "Okay!" he gasped, shaking free of Patrik, eyes so bloodshot he could barely see. "You got it." He took a breath. "Right?"

"Yeah. You win. I got it."

And Patrik left him there and went back to bed.

That night, after work, Taylor opened the cage. He took them out to shower, gave them a clean set of clothes, and taped back George's ear, wrapping a rag around his head.

But it wasn't until after supper when the room was quiet that they talked.

"You're not normal, George, — how you do things. Did you know that?"

"Well, someone had to stop you. What choice did I have?"

They were lying on their cots. It was almost dark.

"I didn't realize how serious it was."

"You acted like Coats was paying you, Patrik. Rest of the team wanted to kill you."

"Shows you how a person can lose touch, think he's all alone out there."

"Well, I lost it too for awhile. Thought you were the enemy."

For a long time no one spoke.

"Nobody's perfect, Patrik. Right?"

Patrik closed his eyes. "Right," he said quietly.

CHAPTER IX

It was three months before they were ready to attempt their first escape. Because everyone knew that they could have taken the warden's car but didn't, what happened that day with the shovel would not be counted against them. According to the warden, justice had been served right at the scene.

This is an important detail because prisoners received nine months added time for each escape, or attempted escape. So later when Patrik figured that after one year at the camp, George's total time had increased to ten and one half years, that was how he figured it.

Although George had been right to say, we have to get away from Coats, he was wrong to assume that Coats could have them transferred if he didn't like the way they worked. From Coats, you couldn't go down; you could only go up. The worst offenders, white as well as black, were assigned to him. He was given no machinery, made no private contracts, accepted no outside money. Obsessed with labor as an end in itself, he drove his men to stupification.

Coats was the first of the captains to come for his men, and the last of the captains to bring them in. Often he came so early, so many hours before dawn, that it was truly the middle of the night. He would bring with him two large trays of breakfast rolls, freshly baked. According to rumor it was Coats' wife, whom nobody had ever seen, who did the baking. But maybe not. Maybe he baked the rolls himself.

Coats was a man of all weathers — nothing could keep him in. If it rained, his men went out to work in the rain. If it began to rain in the middle of a job, they continued to work in the rain all day. If it rained so impossibly that they could not work, they would wait for hours huddled together under a tarp in the back of his truck. If they completed a job at — say, four or five in the afternoon, he would pack them up and drive them to another spot. Under no conditions would they go in before dark.

Coats always wore boots and he always wore a lot of unnecessary clothing — baggy pants, two shirts, a coat and a hat. Ninety degrees didn't faze him. And he never sat in the shade. Maybe he was doing penance. At any rate, his agenda was closed. You just had to live with it.

So they did. They behaved. George, whether working beside Patrik or back in his place at the end of the line, had begun to do his share. Patrik, although still preferring to be out in front, had begun to set a more reasonable pace. They observed Coats. He observed them. They tolerated him, tried to survive him; he did the same. So delicate was this balance, so all-absorbing, that there was time for little else. The months passed. Their wounds healed. And they were going to get the break they had been waiting for.

The man who could engineer their escape, if they could afford it, was a black businessman, an entrepreneur who had made his initial fortune illegally and who, although settled down and respected now, continued to dabble in petty crime as a kind of hobby — the way that some successful men play golf, or go to the trouble to cheat on their wives — in order not to die from boredom.

The proprietor of a popular tavern named after himself, Alfred Rolle supplied his own whiskey, ran a gambling game in the back, and on certain Friday afternoons allowed the men from the camp who had been "contracted out" (leased by the warden to work on private land) to enjoy his facilities with the money they earned. Here they could eat, drink, and purchase supplies.

And for ten dollars they could see a girl.

Rolle also owned a used car lot. Years ago, he had purchased a batch of stolen vehicles from an associate who brought them in from another state. He extended credit to all the poor and put everyone who applied behind the wheel of something.

Still not content, he gave the economy another boost by hiring all the local troublemakers for the inevitable repossessions. He published a list in the local news and paid fifty dollars to whoever brought in the vehicle, no matter who they were or how they got it.

But this was a game of which the town soon tired, and the dusty lot was as full today as the day it had opened, with half of the cars not even running. So tentative was their ownership that no one, including Rolle himself, had been willing to making repairs.

There was, however, a little office on the lot, set off the ground on cinder blocks, and it was in this office late at night that private contracts could still be made, secure behind the wire fencing that surrounded the property.

It was here also, in the small room adjoining the office, that Alfred Rolle could safely hide whatever or whomever needed hiding.

But to get to that room was a long haul. Rolle was a businessman, not a philanthropist.

"Something's up, Patrik." George nudged his friend as Coat's truck made a sudden unexpected turn. "We're going in early."

It was late September, about 5 p.m. The camp road they were now on was an unpaved single lane with ruts and potholes enough to deter any visitor who didn't have it memorized or who wasn't driving a full sized truck. It began at the end of a county road where the pavement broke up in huge uneven blocks, continued for half a mile through thick brush, a few COUNTY PROPERTY, KEEP OUT, NO TRESPASSING signs, and finally an imposing barricade that warned: DANGER EXPLOSIVES.

After this there was a long hill at the crest of which you could view the camp.

A few of the prisoners were standing up. "Truck's in the yard. It's Bates — come to recruit."

Recruit? Patrik and George exchanged a look.

Usually the "teams for hire" were already in place. Prison machinery was used and payment was made to the warden who would then distribute a small portion of this money to the team captains and an even smaller amount to the teams themselves. Occasionally, however, a private company would need laborers only, coming to the camp and selecting the men, assuming all other responsibilities. In these cases, the warden stood to profit most. But the prisoners also received more money or, to be exact, more credit. At Rolle's tavern, it was always credit.

The only ones to whom it would remain a mystery why Bates, who had already chosen the best and strongest from the other teams, was specifically waiting for Coats' truck, would be the camp guards. As usual, most of them didn't get it.

The warden got it — knew that Bates was curious enough about these kids to wait until midnight, if that's what it took.

Coats got it, knew that Bates was here to pull a power play on him. Even the other prisoners got it. "He's here for you," one of them said looking back at George. And then he smiled. "Don't worry. Bates is all right. At least he's a human son-of-a-bitch." He turned then, so that his back was to the cab and sat down on a plank of wood supported by two buckets. For a few seconds he observed George. "Look, he ain't the one," he said quietly. "It's his friend, Alfred Rolle."

"How much."

"Depends. Three … four hundred."

"Damn." George shook his head.

"Don't worry about it," the other prisoner, who was white, looked past George into the yard where Bates stood talking to the warden. George followed his eyes.

"They're all full of shit," the white man was saying. "I wouldn't trust a goddamn one — money or not."

Advise like that, the kind that cancels itself out, is usually good advise with a warning to be careful. So that's how they took it.

And Bates *was* human — hot breakfast on the site, lunch truck coming by eleven. It was all political of course, facing down the warden in front of the entire camp, threatening to cancel the whole deal if Patrik and George weren't part of it, striding up and down like a general, like a bush pilot in his leather coat with his thick grey hair and his cool blue eyes, smelling like expensive after-shave, stopping every now and then to check his watch. He was enjoying the hell out of it.

But the real fun came at the work site. He had to take the sheriff into his trailer to calm him down, had to get him drunk in there. At the time, Patrik and George believed the sheriff was afraid they could escape as Bates had only one man watching them, sitting back up under a tree, shotgun on his lap. They didn't realize it was their age that worried him, the work site being so close to the highway and people always curious when they saw the chains.

"Know who I saw today — watching us from behind the fence?" They were back at the camp. George was sitting on the floor of the cage. "Murdok's twin brother."

Patrik lifted his head. He had been resting on his cot. "Now ... why in hell would you say that?"

"Thought you might like to know." George looked at him.

"What did his car look like?"

"White van."

"How long did he stay?"

"I don't know. Not long."

Patrik lay back again, eyes open. "I thought I saw him myself a few times."

"Patrik?"

"What?"

"How could he know where we are? No one back home knows."

"Maybe he has contacts up here. Someone gave him our description."

"So he came to look? All the way from Florida?"

Patrik was quiet.

"Son of a bitch followed us, Patrik."

"Doesn't matter," Patrik rolled onto his side, closing his eyes. "We won't be here long."

That Friday, for the first time, they went to Rolle's.

"I don't think it's worth the money, George." Patrik looked around. They had been in the tavern for about forty minutes. Most of the men were playing pool, or waiting for a turn to play. "Why not tell the bartender that we need to talk to Mr. Rolle?"

"Because it's not a cool way to do it." George glanced across the room, "What about Hulk over there?" Bates' guard sat at a table like theirs, alone in the corner, watching them.

Patrik sighed. In twenty minutes they would have to go. So far, no sign of Rolle.

"It's not like it's money, Patrik. It's credit." George paused. "We need help, don't we?"

"Well, at least *try* the bartender. Tell him you have an important message." Patrik was studying the bartender. "See what he says. Okay?"

"Yeah. Okay."

But George was lying. If he had learned one thing in his life it was this: if you have a choice, trust a girl.

But he was terribly nervous, hoping she would be young, hoping she would be willing to help them, hoping she would be *able* to help them.

He was so nervous, in fact, that for the first time since Miami he gave his right name. "George Wright" he told the bartender who had pulled out his notebook to write it down. "George R. White," he corrected, watching the bartender add White, striking a line through Wright. 'Damn!' he thought. But no one else would see it. Only Rolle. And Bates.

"Okay. Follow me." The bartender checked his watch. "You've got ten minutes."

So that it was awkward enough — standing there by the heavy black curtain at the end of the dark storeroom; it was pressure enough with the clock ticking that if, for a tenth of a second, the image of Murdok looking through the fence beside the huge blue and white sign: BATES CONSTRUCTION, did cross George's mind, it was gone just as fast.

"It's Sheila ... right?" he said to the bartender. And when he got a nod, and the hint of a smile, he pushed back the curtain. And he was in.

She was his age, thin and brown, standing at the sink, her back to him, washing her arms. He watched. He couldn't move. She was so ... smooth.

She looked up, pausing — suddenly aware. She turned, caught her breath and reached for a towel. Embarrassed, she looked at him accusingly.

He looked at her face. "Hi." He tried not to smile.

"Hi," she looked down, wrapping the towel around her.

"You want me to go back out? So you can ... " There was a brown, satin slip, plain and short, tossed on the bed, "get ready, put on your slip?"

"No, it's all right." She took a quick look at him, smiled, and looked down again. "Come in." She sat on the bed. "Sit here," she said, and patted a place next to her.

So he did.

"You're so young," she was looking at him now, relaxing. "It feels … different."

She took his hand. "You want me to wash you?"

"No, I'll do it."

'I have to stop this,' he was thinking, getting up, moving to the sink, turning on the water. 'All I have to do is be honest, tell her why I'm really here, forget how she looks, don't look at her … stop looking at her.'

So he took a deep breath, turned off the water, and turned to face her. But she was there. And the towel was on the bed. And she was touching him.

It was the gentlest experience he had ever had. And when it was over, and he looked at her, it seemed so easy.

"Can you help us?" he said softly.

She nodded. "Send your mail from here. Let it come here too — the money, whatever you can manage. I'll talk to Mr. Rolle for you."

That Sunday they composed their first letter. It was addressed to Melissa, Patrik's sister who lived in Texas. They reported that all was well and that they were working their way slowly to New York. They asked to borrow two hundred dollars, and they swore Melissa to secrecy whether or not she could send the money.

But here was the problem. If they waited until Friday to mail it, two of their three weeks with Bates would be up. Wouldn't it make more sense to slip the letter to one of the free men on the job site?

Although this last idea bothered George who preferred to keep all white people out of his business, it seemed safer than trusting one of the seminary students (Patrik's idea) who came to the camp each Sunday in black robes and tennis shoes, walking up and down the bunkhouse, passing out pamphlets and trying for converts.

"You'd trust one of them?" George had been observing them. "They'd go right to the warden, Patrik."

"No they wouldn't. I don't even care if they do. It's an innocent letter, George. That's all it is."

82

"Innocent, my ass. Two hundred dollars worth of F-ing innocent, my ass."

So they sent it on Monday with one of Bates' men.

The next Friday, in order not to arouse suspicion, George sent Patrik back to see Sheila. I'll see her next week," he had said. "Go on, Patrik. It's okay. She's nice."

Sheila, wearing a slip, was sitting on the bed.

"Hi, I'm Patrik. George's friend."

"Hi, come and sit down."

He sat down but not too close. "There's some money coming from Texas, from my sister. It's addressed to you. I don't know how much." He looked at her. "Can you help us?"

"It's up to Mr. Rolle. He said he'll consider it," she paused, "because, you know, you just want to go home."

"Right. Well, no. Just out of state. North. My sister lives … " But the thing about going home had thrown him so he was trying to recover, looking down, measuring his words, "She lives in Virginia, so we just basically need a ride to where she can pick us up."

He took a breath. What was that about? Why confuse things? Virginia could be home — couldn't it? He could have two sisters — one in Texas and one in Virginia. What was he doing?

"It's all right." Sheila was watching him. She smiled suddenly, putting a hand on his arm, leaning towards him so that he was forced to look at her. "He's done it before."

"And no one suspects him?"

"They can't do anything to him. He's their friend. But … no, they don't suspect. I don't think they suspect."

"Next week is our last chance to see you."

"I know. You may have to get away from the camp yourselves. Next Saturday would be best. Can you do that?"

"Sure. Good." He nodded, looking up at her intently. "No problem."

She smiled. "Do you want to lay down with me?"

She had begun to stroke his arm.

Patrik stood. "No. Not now. I … couldn't." He looked back at her. How old was she … fifteen? … fourteen?

George had said sixteen. But no, she was younger than that.

"Look," he watched her as he spoke. "Maybe there's something *you* would like. Is there?"

She stood up, self-conscious, smoothing her slip. "You know what I would like? You won't laugh?"

"Of course not." Patrik had to smile. She looked so ... innocent standing there barefoot, deciding whether or not she was going to trust him.

"Can you hear the music?"

Patrik listened. From the jukebox in the bar a love song was playing. "You want to dance?" He took her hand. "That's it?"

So they danced, slowly. And Patrik remembered Lorraine. And he understood Sheila and it hurt him to understand her.

And he understood George a little better too.

They never did meet Alfred Rolle. He had seen them of course, and on the third Friday he discussed them with Bates, sitting in his office with the door closed.

"What don't sit right with me, Bates, is this. Where's their kin? We all know it's wrong — kids like that. Why don't their families come up here and appeal the damn thing?"

"Maybe kin don't know."

"Well now, that ain't so smart, is it? The darker one calls himself — James." Rolle reached over and pulled Bates' clipboard closer, "Patrik James, is that it?"

Bates nodded.

Rolle studied the list of names from the camp. "And the other one is ... Russell? He compared the names with those scrawled on the bartender's pad. "Now which is it, Bates? George Russell or George White?"

Bates was quiet.

"This darker one," Rolle continued, "says he's got a sister in Virginia. So ... where is she?" he looked up.

Bates didn't answer. "Wait and see, Al," he said finally. "Somebody's going to show up sooner or later."

But maybe they already had.

Rolle waited until Bates and his team were gone. He came out of his office, went into the bar and sat down at one of the tables. The bartender brought him a glass of ice.

"Wait. Sit down. Anything more on the van?"

"Not lately." The bartender glanced around the room, " ... seen him parked out in the woods the other night."

"When was that?"

"Two days ago. I took a flashlight, tried to talk to him. Son-of-a bitch hides his face. Says he's here to do some fishin."

"Fishin or huntin?"

"Fishing. Knows about the dam."

"He's come a long damn way to go fishing — now, aint he? Know what he's got in the back of that van?"

"Couldn't tell. No windows back there."

"Send someone to find out." Rolle reached into his pocket, pulled out a thick roll of bills and peeled off two twenties. "I don't want him here Saturday night. Do you follow me? I want him gone."

Then he took out a fifty, folded it and placed it under his glass. "These two young boys ... from the camp. What do you think?"

"Nice kids. They're okay, Al."

"Good." Rolle pushed back his chair. "I'll need you here Saturday night. Tell me if you need more money."

But he didn't like it. He didn't like the timing of it. Some damn investigator from Florida — or worse, one of those slimy federal agents with an arsenal in his van camping out in the woods.

Rolle sat back heavily in his chair. Maybe he'd help these kids but not yet. He didn't know enough about them. He didn't know a damn thing about them.

Slowly he got to his feet. Better put the whole thing off. Next week, when they came in with Bates, he'd talk to them personally, clear a few things up. Maybe he'd tell them he'd had a call from Florida, see what their reaction was.

But Rolle had forgotten something. There wasn't going to be another week with Bates. The contract was up.

CHAPTER X

They decided to play sick. Prisoners hung on the fence were taken down around 4 p.m., before the other men returned from work.

"Taylor," Patrik had said that morning. "Take the key with you." Taylor hesitated. The cage door, open since Coats had left without them, was rarely locked during the day. Its key, on a nail by the bunkhouse door, was used only at night.

"The warden's got a key, Patrik. If he wants to come in here and lock you down, he will." Taylor looked into the cage at George. "How sick is he?"

"Pissed blood last night. Will you take the key?"

Taylor sighed. "All right. I'll tell the warden about the blood." And he tucked the key into his clothes.

At eight a.m., Watkins and one other guard entered the bunkhouse with shotguns, ordering Patrik and George to the fence. The warden, remembering what Taylor had told him, personally oversaw the entire ritual, excusing George from the castor oil and instructing the guards to leave him alone. He kept an eye on them, though, trying to guess what they planned to do next.

Some wardens actually earn their salaries this way — guarding the guards. Because, you see, they're tricky — like kids. You can't leave them alone for a goddamn minute! Say you have some business — a dental appointment, for example. God only knows what they'll do while you're gone.

But the warden was in luck that day. By mid-morning it had started to rain, a cold, driving, slanted rain that would fill the yard with rivers of mud. If this kept up, it was safe to go. He might even stop at Rolle's for a while. Why not? No one would come to the camp today.

He was right. The guards settled down to play cards. The phone didn't ring. And on and off all day it rained.

The warden left at noon. On the chance it would still be raining when he returned, he left the front gate open.

"Hey, Patrik, is the courtyard locked?"

Patrik shook his head. It was almost three o'clock and the rain had temporarily stopped.

"Are you sure?"

Patrik tried to remember if Taylor had locked the courtyard gate. If not, once back in the bunkhouse they could exit over the courtyard wall and down along the back of Bunkhouse Two. "Don't worry about it," he said finally, meaning at this point it didn't matter. They had options. They'd do whatever they had to do.

"Watkins!" Watkins was sloshing across the yard. "You going to take us in?" Watkins looked them over. This was the second time he had crossed the yard.

"He can't find Taylor's key." George looked at Patrik. "Warden must have his with him. "If there's a third one, we'll find out now."

But they never did find out because when Watkins came back for them, shotgun in hand, he wasn't talking. He uncuffed Patrik, watched while Patrik uncuffed George, then prodded them towards the bunkhouse door.

"You go in first." Patrik looked sideways at George. "I'll hold him."

"Right." George looked back towards the front gate. Still open.

"Watkins, look here. Get us some towels. Will you do that?" Patrik stood in the doorway, Watkins behind him. He glanced towards George who had moved into the room ahead of him. George looked back. The courtyard was locked.

"Watkins, we need some heat in here. You going to fire up some heat for us?"

But Watkins wasn't coming in that room. He stepped back, raising his shotgun suspiciously. "Go to the cage." He nudged Patrik with the gun, moving him out of the doorway. "Both of you. In the cage."

Damn! They hadn't wanted to do it this way — not out in the yard, not in plain view of the office! But Watkins was behind the door now, pushing it closed.

"Let's get him." They moved together going all the way back with the door that Watkins had stepped behind. And Watkins was hit hard, carried with it, slammed between the door and the side of the building.

So there they were, in the yard, with Watkins pinned behind the door. They waited. Nothing. They lightened up, just a fraction. Watkins crumpled, his body pushing against them.

"You want to drag him inside?" Patrik stepped back releasing the door completely. George did the same. It creaked, moved several inches, and stopped.

Watkins slid down noisily. One of his shoes appeared under the door.

"Hell, no. Do you?"

Scrambling now, right past the office, right through the open front gate, pulling up their chains as the cold wind whipped their clothes, ducking down and running, hunched over like crabs in the high weeds.

It was a long hill. Tunneling up and up through the undergrowth, chains in their hands, their line of ascent growing thinner and thinner as they burrowed into the thick brush.

Only once did they look back, stopping to rest at the top of the hill, forgetting the story of Lot, the superstition of prisoners everywhere that if you look back you're going back.

And the door to the bunkhouse was still ajar. And the room in which they had been caged stared vacantly at them, looking small and fowl in the muddy yard, like a darkening wound, like a dead man ... like a toothless mouth.

The warden was still at Rolle's when the call came from the camp. In fact he was drunk, sitting back in Rolle's office helping himself to a bottle of rum. The bartender took the call, checked his watch, waited for about fifteen minutes and made some coffee.

He knocked on the office door. "The camp's looking for the warden," he said simply. "I told them I'd let you know."

Sometimes a person needs a little push. Rolle knew this was the day. He was prepared for it but he was not committed to it. The truth is, he had tried to stop it. "Can you get a message out to the camp?" he had asked a friend who ran deliveries out there for the prisoners.

"Message to who?"

"Prisoner named James — Patrik James. It's personal."

"Not until Sunday. Sunday I can do it."

"Sunday's too late. How about tomorrow?"

"Nope, can't do it. Be gone to work — all of them."

So that was the end of it.

But now, as Rolle realized what his bartender was telling him, as it struck him that here sat the warden comfortably drunk in the same room to which his escaped prisoners were headed, as the truly delicious irony of it lit up his soul, Rolle was in — he couldn't pass it up.

Actually, the tavern would be their final stop. They were to wait at the car-lot (Sheila had drawn them a little map) most of the night. By then the truck with Rolle's whiskey safely unloaded would be anxious to start its trip back home; destination: Charlotte, N.C.

"So what do you think their chances are, Al?" It was eight o'clock. Bates had come into the tavern, ordered himself a steak and a bottle of scotch, and then, like the rest of the town, just sat there waiting.

It was like a damn hurricane party.

"Not good, Bates." Rolle sat down heavily.

"Well I hope they don't go north. Ed Cusick's got those dogs of his right shy of County line. He'll start 'em right from there — it's worked before."

Bates paused. He poured himself a drink. "The only chance these kids have got, Al, is coming here." He looked at his friend. "You figured out yet what to do with 'em?"

"I'd send 'em home if I knew where it was."

"Where do you think it is?"

"It ain't Virginia; I know that much." Rolle signaled the bar for another glass. He remembered the white van. "Florida, maybe." He looked up. "I'd hate to see them get killed, Bates. But I'll tell you the truth. I don't know what their story is. Do you follow? I don't know what in hell these kids are running from."

The arrangement was this: they would stay on the land until well after midnight. Then, creeping down one of the back streets from the woods north of town, they would find the car-lot, lock themselves in, locate the wire running under the door and plug it in. This wire activated the streetlight and would signal Rolle that they were there.

What they didn't realize was that by keeping them away for hours, Rolle could be sure that no one knew which way they had gone. Otherwise, they would have been caught.

"So, where do you plan to hide them, Al?" It was ten o'clock. The sheriff had been to the tavern twice by now, rounding up more men, more trucks, more beer. Rolle and Bates had moved to the office. "They know about the car-lot?"

Rolle didn't answer.

"You might as well do something useful with it." Bates was feeling a little drunk. "You ain't sold a car there since '58."

"I sold 'em." Rolle leaned across his desk. "I got one old dodge out there that I sold thirteen times." He lowered his voice. "This is the last time I'm doing this, Bates, if I do it at all — which I may not. My car-lot ain't a damn motel, you know."

"Sure it is. Remember those white boys?"

"I remember. Almost died on us — drank swamp water."

"Well you'd better hope these two don't make the same mistake. Or you got hell on your hands," Bates paused, suppressing a smile, "when they show up at that there place of yours, that ain't a motel."

Rolle crossed the tavern parking lot and stood in the dark, waiting for Bates' truck to disappear. He took a long piss in the grass beside his car. 'Florida kids know all about swamps,' he said to himself. 'They ain't stupid.'

Rolle was tired. He got into his car, pushed back the seat and began to doze. After a few minutes he rolled down the window and turned the ignition. Although it was October, the air conditioner in the long black Bonneville hummed steadily. 'They work with Coats, don't they?' he was thinking, opening his eyes, checking the clock, closing them again. 'And nobody told them not to drink the water in those bogs out there?'

That's right, Rolle. Nobody told them.

But they didn't drink much. They had been thirsty for hours, moving in terror across the dark fields, unable to get their chains off, fearful of all human sounds.

"Maybe we should have gone north," George had said, "hid in one of those barns up there."

"He's got our money, George. We tried the other way. Remember?"

And they *had* tried the other way, inching close as they dared to a shed, a barn, creeping through the brown grass while they watched for lights in the house nearby. But then a dog would bark — a lone yelp, sharp and clear, stopping them, driving them back with a life-sapping dread, terribly afraid to be caught like this, shot down in the weeds, in the dark, in the dirt.

It was four a.m. when Rolle stirred, shook himself and checked the clock on the dashboard. He turned off the air conditioner, pulled on his parking lights, and slid the Bonneville out of the driveway. The streets were empty and the light outside the car-lot was on.

The boys lay on the floor. "Wake up," he prodded George first, then Patrik. Slowly he shone his flashlight up and down the length of each of them. Again, more intently. They looked bad — very bad.

With an effort, he reached down and shook the second boy's shoulder. He felt his face. Fever. He looked back at George, aiming the beam of light directly on his forehead, his neck. This one too — drenched with it.

Rolle straightened, settling his weight back onto his hips. He clicked off the flashlight. It wouldn't do. It wouldn't do at all. Taking some blankets from the single empty cot against the wall he covered them carefully and walked into the other room.

For several minutes Rolle sat behind his desk, in the little office in the dark. Suppose, against all of his instincts, he sent them north, across the state line. What did they know of the land up there? They were already sick. He'd never known anyone personally who died from drinking swamp water but he'd heard of such a thing.

Even worse, suppose the trucker noticed how sick they were, started asking questions? Fever could make them delirious, start them babbling.

Rolle turned on the shaded lamp next to the telephone on his desk. He took out the envelope that Sheila had given him — two hundred dollars. It wasn't enough. The risk was too high. Perhaps next time their friend from Texas could send more money. Or the sister from Virginia could pay him a visit, arrange to pick them up herself.

Alfred Rolle felt no remorse when he picked up the phone to call the camp. In fact, he felt greatly relieved, felt like a new man.

Well, it happens. We get old. We decide to cover our own asses.

CHAPTER XI

Although Patrik and George were recaptured without incident, the warden didn't like what happened next. He didn't do much about it, but at least he didn't like it.

He decided to keep them outside, attached to the fence, for seventy-two hours. They were going to be beaten; there was no way to stop it. But he could set limits, check on them every morning when he came to work, make sure the guards did nothing that might show up later if they went to court.

In his opinion, the beatings were an embarrassment to the camp. They were stupid, a waste of time — recreation for a bunch of misfits. But what could he do? You see, the warden's hours were from six to six. He wasn't at the camp at night.

And the beatings were bad.

So bad in fact, so brutal, with such a variety of shouts and raucous laughter from the guards, that the men in the bunkhouse would begin to pace around and listen. "Good God Almighty," one of them would mumble. And then it would be silent for a while. THUMP, they would hear. THUMPTHUMP.

" ...Damn!" another would say, "how much of this are we supposed to take?"

It was usually Connors who borrowed Taylor's chair but sometimes Smith or Dobbs would do it. They would stand on this chair and pull themselves up to the top of the wall, looking out the narrow ventilation space below the roof until the boys were dragged back down the steps again and returned to the fence for the rest of the night.

"They'll be all right," Smith said, at the end of the second night. "I'd hate for one of us to have to kill somebody over this."

"Why don't we pull one of them guards in here," Connors suggested, "hold him hostage, make a deal with him?"

"Leave it alone," Dobbs said. "Ain't nothing going to happen to those kids they can't survive. I'm watching them. They're tough."

Well, they tried. They tried to be tough. The weakness, the degradation of their position, they could handle. They were sick but after all they had been sick before. The threats, the intimidations, the vivid descriptions of how these guards were going to kill them, how they would be dismembered, buried, how their murders would be covered up, they knew that this was just a trick.

But although they knew this, they couldn't remember their own tricks. They should have some defense — all the shit they'd been through in their lives.

It's rough, though, in a situation like this. As far as the actual pain goes, you're going to have to take it. You can't pass out; you can't allow yourself the luxury. One of the ways to keep track of things is to focus on a certain face — never the face of the man who beats you, the face of someone who is watching him beat you. And the eyes of this man become a mirror so that both of you are watching the same thing, as if it were a film. And, strangely, you can understand the boredom of your witness with this film, his slow disgust. And you can almost count the minutes till the audience walks out.

Until the film is over and the theater is dark. But strangely, you can still hear. And then slowly you realize that no one has walked out at all. No one has left. The darkened theater is full.

And you can hear the movements of the men around you, hear their footsteps, hear them breathing over you, hear the sudden silence when the breathing stops and the door slams and they are gone.

Strange the way this darkness continues — later, days later, aching and feverish under that damn woolen blanket, waking up sweaty and smelly, moving carefully onto your side, unable to find a single position where something doesn't hurt. You know, for example, that the beatings are over. You know that you are safe now, back in the cage. But if this is true, then who is that on the floor of the bunkhouse? He is lying so still, and all the other men are sitting on their cots just watching him.

And then, with creeping horror you begin to realize that the guards are there too, in that same room, in that same darkness. They begin to emerge and to slowly circle the form that is you. But the form doesn't move.

And you yell from the cage but no one can hear you, and you can't get out. You are terrified now, terrified at what the guards are going to do. And then one of them leans down and straddles the form on the floor. He is … riding it. He is *riding* it!

And your heart pounds and you struggle to sit up. 'Jesus,' you think, 'what's happening to me? *What's happening to me?*'

"George. Can you hear me?"

"I can hear you."

"F-ing nightmares are hell, man."

"I'm hip."

Patrik let out a long breath. "What time is it?"

George lifted his head. "It's … maybe it's around eight … around nine, something like that."

"Damn, it's hot. Why is it so F-ing hot!

"I keep going back over what they did."

"Stay awake. Don't sleep."

Patrik looked out through the bars of the cage. Slowly he got up, moved to the end of the cage and felt around for the bucket of water. "No light," he was mumbling, "can't see shit in here." He picked up the bucket and tried to pour some water into the basin, but the water spilled.

"TAYLOR," he threw the bucket down, spilling the rest of the water; the bucket clanged against the side of the cage.

"WE NEED WATER." He was holding onto the sink, looking out into the shadowed room. "I'm SICK. I need WATER."

Taylor emerged from the darkness. "You get more water tomorrow. I can give you a cup of water — to drink. You want that?"

Patrik didn't answer. He looked at Taylor.

"I can't unlock the cage, warden's orders. Tomorrow night, if you're quiet, maybe I can let you out. You can take a shower."

Patrik looked beyond Taylor. A few of the men were still awake, sitting up smoking, but most had bedded down for the night. No one was talking. No one was moving.

"WHAT IS THIS? A GRAVEYARD? IS EVERYBODY DEAD? ARE YOU ALL DEAD?"

"They're going to come in here with a hose, Patrik, if you don't shut up. You want a hose turned on you, like a dog?"

Taylor looked down the cage. "I put food in there for you, on the floor. And coffee — you can drink that."

"I'll tell you what I can do," Patrik began walking back to his cot. He was talking to himself but loud enough for everyone to hear. "I can blow the dam up, that's what I can do — end everybody's misery.

"They think I don't know where that dynamite is hid,"

He stopped beside his cot, sat down heavily and then slowly lay down on his back. " ... George?"

"You're all right, Patrik."

"No I'm not." He closed his eyes. "Six more years of this I'll be ... I'll be ..."

But something was happening to him now, a shape was moving behind his eyes, crawling, gathering skin and bones. He was not asleep. It was not a dream. And yet, he could see it. So present was Patrik in the cage while he watched this scene, that he was simultaneously aware of his own voice, what he was saying, and every move the creature in his mind was making.

"They want an animal, don't they?" he said to George.

He was looking at a quarry. Some crude machinery, discarded stone — slabs of flawed granite, lay at the bottom. The far wall of the pit was cliff-like, filled with caves. Trees grew out of crevices, hiding the cave entrances. A strange shape made its way along the cliff.

"I'd live in the woods up there ... in those caves. I'd live with that dynamite up there."

Patrik watched the shape ascend from the quarry. He began to follow it. Who was this creature — was it he himself? No, this animal — this ... man was older than Patrik, much older, long grey hair matted into clumps.

And then, at the top of the pit, the figure stood and the coat he was wearing billowed out behind him, and he disappeared. And in the distance Patrik heard the dam.

Patrik opened his eyes. "George?" he spoke softly.

"Yeah."

"Murdok's here. He's at the dam."

George rolled over on his side. "You saw him?"

"He's come to kill me." Patrik sat up.

George came down from his cot. He crouched on the floor next to Patrik.

"Listen, Patrik, I think there's another key."

"Where?"

"Up there," George indicated the top of the cage. "The guards were messing around up there last time they locked us up. I think they stashed an extra key up there."

Patrik got up. He looked out around the room. He moved against the bars, put his arm through and tried to reach the top of the cage. With his fingers he felt along the edge. He moved a little farther down, towards the door.

"Look here," George moved beside him. I made a hook — piece of wire from the bunk."

"Let me see it," Patrik had reached the cage door. He pulled himself up on the door and stretched his arm completely through the bars. He positioned himself sideways and slid the hook along the top of the cage.

"Wait until tomorrow," George stood below him. "You want someone to hear you, see what you're doing?"

Patrik came back down, pulling his arm into the cage. Out of breath, he looked at George. "I got it," he said.

Well, it was going to be a long, long night. Dobbs got up once, lit half a cigarette, smoked it and lay down again. Connors' radio played for hours, haunting music, the saxophone of the old South — not of cities but of the rivers and the rain. Finally he turned it off. But the feeling stayed thick in the room, like a scent.

"You know what I don't understand?" George lay on his side. "Why are we worried about them?"

It was completely quiet.

"I mean, they're prisoners too."

"Too friendly with the guards. Always talking to them, smuggling things in and out."

"You wouldn't even trust Connors?"

"Nope. Smith neither. Only person ever gave a single shit about us was Sheila. And maybe that white guy told us about Rolle; wasn't his fault how it worked out."

For a few seconds George was silent. "Here's what I want to know. Why was that key up there?"

Patrik didn't answer.

"See what I mean? Every day since we've been back, guards keep comin in here, walking around ... walking around. If Taylor locked the courtyard gate, they unlock it. What's the point of that? And the key for the cage right over our heads?"

"You think they want us to find it?"

"I think it's possible."

"I don't care," Patrik lay back down, "even if they do."

For a while they lay there, each alone, thinking.

"Patrik, we should wait. Let things cool down."

"You wait. I can't. I meant it — what I said about the dam."

"Bullshit you did. Stop talking crazy, Patrik. Turn the set off."

"Can't do it."

"Sure you can. Think about Lorraine."

For a few seconds Patrik didn't answer. "She's gone," he said quietly. "can't find her anymore."

"She'll come back. Focus on her," George was still on his side. He lifted his head, propping himself up a few inches. "Remember how she smells. Just go with it.

"You don't need to *see* her, Patrik. Follow me?"

"I need to see if Murdok's at the dam. That's what I need to see."

For several minutes they were quiet. George lowered his voice then, speaking in a tone that was just above a whisper. "Patrik, we need to file our chains down before we try it again. Get them nice and thin." He paused. "Remember last time?"

"I don't care about the chains."

George didn't answer. In the darkness, Smith coughed.

And then, once more, it was silent.

"You don't understand, George; I'm at that point. If they kill me, good. Either way, it's over. I'm out."

George waited for a few minutes. When he spoke it was so softly that Patrik hardly heard him. "That's where I was coming from too, that day with the shovel. It wasn't just about you. Remember that day?"

"I remember." Patrik closed his eyes.

"So tomorrow we go." George lay on his back. "Right?"

"Right. Tomorrow. "

Of course everyone had heard the whole thing, so that an hour before dawn when Taylor quietly slipped out and disappeared, several of the other men got up also and dressed quietly.

And when the warden's car slowed, approaching the front gate, Smith and Connors were waiting in the yard for him.

And Coats went out of his way that day — a thing he'd never done before, to stop at a place where there was a phone.

In Bunkhouse One, everything went as predicted. The men left for work; the guards came and went, sliding the heavy bar across the outside door but leaving the courtyard gate unlocked. The cage opened easily; they re-hid the key.

They decided to gather a few supplies before they left. George had been right; they needed a file. It was a strange feeling though, going through the other prisoners' things, socks and underwear, photographs and letters. They couldn't find the file anywhere; strange because they had seen Smith with it just yesterday.

However, Taylor had a scissors so they took that, and Connors had two dollars in the back of his radio. They stole a pack of matches from Dobbs. But there was something degrading about what they were doing, so they let it go at that: the scissors, the matches, and the money.

They moved into the courtyard. It was mid-October, cool and crisp with a pale sky and a clean, outlined look to everything — as if they were walking through a picture, a place where every thing was smaller, less threatening than they had remembered it, a place that was already fixed in time, like a memory.

To scale the courtyard wall was difficult because several strands of barbed wire lay along the top of it. Although more noisy, if they could get onto the corrugated tin roof above the kitchen, they could easily get over the barbed wire. Also, they'd be able to see the ground — the narrow passageway along the wall. And they could see the front of the prison too. By standing, they could see everything — all the way to the camp road.

The roof was eighteen feet long, eight feet wide, and shaky. It stood seven feet high, covered an ancient cast iron stove, a free-standing oven, a long table and a metal cabinet. This was the kitchen, gated and locked. George took the easy way, climbing up the gate, then pulling himself onto the roof from there, pausing when most of his body was on the roof, his legs dangling.

Patrik used one of the posts next to the wall to accomplish the same result, scrambling onto the roof and crouching there while he waited for George. Cautiously he peered through the four strands of barbed wire. Someone was down there.

George was making his way along the roof. Patrik signaled him to keep low, to be quiet, but it was too late. The roof indented, popped out, indented again.

George stopped. From the front of the complex, a guard whistled a sharp whistle, the way you call a dog when you don't have time for the long version.

Patrik looked through the wire. The guard who had been standing directly below him was running towards the front of the building, his shotgun under his arm.

Patrik moved closer to the edge, partially standing.

Two more guards — both running, not looking up.

Patrik stood upright. He turned, looking over the courtyard towards the front of the camp. So stunned was the expression on his face that George, who had almost reached him, straightened and began to turn around to see what he was looking at but never got the chance because suddenly Patrik noticed him, grabbed his arm, and pulled him down again.

"George. Don't move. The whole F-ing world is out there." He crouched down beside him.

George stared at him.

"They're on horses. Dozens of them."

George turned and stood slowly. The camp road was full of men, men on horseback, men with hats, long hair. 'Coats?' he thought incredulously. He looked down into the yard. The sheriff's car was at the gate. The warden was on a horse, his pistol drawn; one guard stood in front of him, arms up, shotgun on the ground. Three other guards appeared, put down their shotguns, and raised their arms.

George looked back at Patrik. "Well, look at this," he said simply, "it's a bust."

CHAPTER XII

It was evening. A week had passed since the incident with the horses and although the boys had not been, would never be, addressed directly about it, all eyes had turned to them as they stood in their chains on the kitchen roof while the sheriff arrested, cuffed, and shoved into his car the four guards who had planned to kill them.

"Planned to shoot 'em down like birds," Taylor had said, later that night speaking to Connors, "soon as they jumped."

They were out in the courtyard with the other men, lined up behind Connors, waiting for supper.

"That's right," Taylor had continued, "drop 'em just like wild geese."

"Young boys took a risk, all right," Connors had answered. "But they did good." And then he had smiled. "Looks like we got our camp back."

Approval can have a dramatic effect. In fact, it can be so productive it's a wonder social structures are so tight with it. Nature approves. Trees don't require certain conditions be met before we can sit in their shade.

Like the college kid with his resume, maybe we all deserve a shot at the top. It's just that it's easier to prove this after we've got it.

Which is exactly what happened with Patrik and George.

The event had been rewritten in their favor. They endorsed it. They admired it. They were even beginning as the days passed to look around for more things to endorse and to admire. For example, Connors. Of course they could trust him — had they been crazy?

You see, it's all reciprocal. So when Connors looked right at them after a lull in the conversation (they were sitting at the long table in the bunkhouse after supper,) when Connors zeroed in on them like that, bringing up the subject of their next escape as calmly as he would have mentioned — say, the weather, it shouldn't have produced the shock that it did.

"When do you think would be the best time, Smith, for these boys we've got here to try it again?" Smith and Connors were drinking coffee. Taylor had left the room and the men were alone.

"A month at best. Maybe two."

Smith looked first at George, then at Patrik. He was probably in his early fifties, small and skinny. Five times he had tried to catch a certain payroll at the local train station, and five times he had been left empty handed. Foiled each time by a woman friend who, in Smith's words, "never even read the Constitution because if she did she would have known that Church and State is separate, and you don't save somebody's soul by busting him. You don't call the sheriff so he can alert the company so they can change the schedule. It ain't American."

Smith's current plan was this: He would slip away from the camp one night, rob the station, bury the money and return to camp. He wasn't even going to wear a mask, just walk right in and announce himself. To Smith, his reputation was his gold. Of course the sheriff and the warden felt the same way but Smith couldn't help that.

"I'm a contented man," Smith would say, "a happy man." And he'd laugh. "Know why? Cuz I'm smarter 'n all of 'em."

Patrik looked steadily at Smith. Your vision clears up in prison; all of your senses become more acute. Sometimes you can go right down inside a person's eyes — directly to that tiny window way back in there, mirrored and glittering.

It's quite an event for anyone — the first time that he sees that shutter flash, the first time that he sees the brilliant vortex to a universe he never even guessed was there. It makes a person stop and think for a minute. Or maybe, for more than a minute.

"Have to wait until the ground freezes up," Smith was looking at Connors now. "And even then, best to wait for a good freeze — wait until the lines are frozen too.

"After Christmas," and he picked up his cup, drained it and put it down. "Guards get good and drunk around here come New Year."

So there was nothing to do but wait. And work. They were now assigned permanently to Coats. And Coats hadn't changed. Not only did he keep them well away from human contact, confining them to the thickest of the woods and swamps, he gave them the same backbreaking work as before.

Until it seemed to them that Coats was truly inhuman, truly the devil himself with his crazy assortment of clothes, watching them from the roof of his truck, his glass eye glinting at them in the sun.

And they worked until every muscle screamed for rest, worked to an exhaustion so complete that they could neither eat nor bathe, falling down on their cots the moment they reached them. The older men would save some soup for them on nights like these, some vegetables and bread, and often they would have these for breakfast.

November closed; the year began to die. They were well.

It was the first week in December before the ground began to freeze. Patrik would awaken early now, earlier than ever before. He would sit up on his cot, blow some warmth into his hands, and then reach up and shake the springs above him. "Get up, man!" he would say, standing, slapping George across the legs.

He would wash then, letting the icy water roll all over him. And he'd be ravenously hungry, hollering to Taylor, "Start the coffee, Pops! Let's roll!"

And "Hey, Coats!" he'd yell, "you're late!" — whatever time Coats got there.

Sometimes Patrik was the only one awake, wide awake as the truck pulled out, perfectly aware of every sound, amazed that the other prisoners could sleep, nudging George.

He was entranced by it — the shock of cold air into his lungs, the ice that lay like cellophane across the road, the peculiar lightness of his own weight. He had never seen anything like it, the shaggy coats of animals as if some school child had drawn them.

The children themselves were right out of a book, right off of a calendar, wearing scarves and boots, waving to him as if there were nothing strange at all about his being there, riding across their grey fields.

But he was far from home. Farther than they could ever know. He was hundreds and hundreds of miles from Lorraine, and farther than that from the youth he had lost, from Calvin who also watched the growing light, resting on the steps in front of his door, sandals kicked off, relieved that he had made it through another night. How far was Patrik from him now? Rain, pouring like tears on Miami's streets — so warm. Love is over for another night. Another child. Another life. Weep, Miami. Go to sleep.

But there are times. And there are seasons. For Patrik, the routine of his life now, the stark simplicity of it, agreed with him on a level that was deeply personal. He began to think ... why run?

He didn't mention this to anyone, not even to George. But it was obvious.

One day when they were putting in a bridge, waist-high in water, a moccasin slid across their legs. Patrik grabbed for it, then Dobbs and Connors, but it was young and fast, slithering through the brown water, causing shouts of alarm as Miller slipped, went down, and the snake was lost.

Coats had been watching from above. He stood, raising his shotgun. "Move aside, goddamn it!" And then he carefully took aim, fired, and hit it. And baggy clothes and all, he went right into the river to retrieve it.

Well, it was an event. Everyone stopped working, coming around to remark on the snake, to examine it. Coats built a fire right on the spot, something he rarely did, allowing the men to dry off and relax. For George, it was a chance to rest and he lay next to the fire, closing his eyes.

But for Patrik, it was a different kind of opportunity.

For the first time he began to listen — intently, to the conversations around him. And he began to open from a place so far within himself time seemed reversed, so he could learn.

They were discussing snakes at first, but Patrik's questions led them back and back until they taught him how to read the sky — pale now, ivory with winter, and how to see snow in the low clouds and smell it in the dark slate of a bitter night; how to see ice in a man's breath, hear it in the footsteps of an animal, predict it in flames that crackle violet-blue and trees so brittle their bark, on the underside, is as white as the bones of death itself.

They sat there for almost an hour. And it occurred to Patrik that Coats had almost smiled today, almost been proud about the snake, almost answered him once or twice himself. And he realized that Coats had no friends — not one, among the other officers and guards. And he wondered if his glass eye hurt him, and he wondered if he were ashamed of it.

It was December 24th. And as the talk around the fire continued Patrik felt himself lighten, and slip, and relax into his life.

'I never want to die,' he thought quietly. 'No matter how bad it gets, no matter what anyone tries to tell me, I never want to die.'

The next day, Christmas, Coats delivered to his team, personally, hot biscuits and turkey from his own table. He brought gravy in two large dairy containers, and buttered carrots and greens.

"You're a fine team," he told them, "the finest team I ever had." That was all he said, but for Coats perhaps there wasn't any more than that — no greater compliment was possible. And when he left the men ate quietly. And nobody made fun of Coats that day.

So for Patrik, Christmas passed peacefully and the year drew to a close. With good behavior his six years could be completed in four. Perhaps he could make it.

One should not, however, assume too much. And one should never, no matter how delightfully his own affairs are going, take for granted the agreement of a friend.

"The truth is, Patrik," they were standing by the courtyard gate watching the snow fall in huge silent flakes; tomorrow would be New Year's Eve, " ... the truth is I think you've changed. This is no joke. You're slipping back into that military mode. I can't even talk to you, man."

Patrik glanced at his friend, assessed the fact that he hadn't heard from Sheila this week, and turned his back to watch the snow. "F you," he said.

"Well, I wouldn't bother if it weren't for all we'd been through together."

There was something about the tone of his voice.

Patrik looked at him again. "You're going somewhere?"

"Tomorrow."

"You're crazy. You'll freeze your ass off." Patrik paused. "You can't be serious. You mean this?"

"Would I say it if I didn't mean it?"

"How do I know if you'd say it?"

"Patrik," George looked away, "the point is I'm asking if you want to come. Are you in, or not?"

"Coats will kill you — run you down with his truck."

"Not if the tires are flat. You'll do it?"

Patrik nodded. His eyes scanned the room. "Who else is going?"

"No one from here; other side, new white guy." George looked back at Patrik. "He's from Canada, got his own trans. He has a woman friend who can hide us."

"Does the woman friend know about you?"

"How could she know about me? He just met me himself."

Patrik sighed, "You decided fast on this." He looked down. "I didn't expect it."

George shrugged. "The opportunity came up." And then he just stood there, looking exactly the way he had looked that morning in Miami on his grandmother's porch. "It's better this way, Patrik. We're not married, you know."

They went the next morning — George and the Canadian. Everyone helped. By nightfall they had not been caught. Nor the next day. Nor the one after that.

CHAPTER XIII

"Well they're long gone now," Connors was saying, "long gone out of this damn state." It was the third night.

"You got that right." Dobbs sighed deeply. "Smith, you still awake?"

"I'm layin right here prayin for 'em same as you," Smith paused, "same as every man can hear my voice."

The room was quiet then.

"Amen to that," someone answered. "Amen to that."

They were keeping watch. Prisoners always keep watch when one of them escapes. They do it before an execution too. It doesn't matter who the prisoner is or what he has done to arrive at this point. Mistakes float down like leaves — unnoticed beside the magnitude of extinction.

Could you not watch one hour with me? We understand.

We have been waiting for a long time. Since the beginning. We wait at hospitals. We wait at the window. We wait in the dark.

"The smallest thing that crawls, under the grass," Miller spoke softly, "He don't forget.

"He's out there with 'em, ain't He, Smith?"

"He is," Smith answered. "Yes He is. I have a good feeling about it tonight."

But they all did. Just being cautious, longing to savor what the two might be doing — having a drink maybe, or a long sweet cigarette. Riding along. Or eating ... ahhh, sitting down to a fat steak, or a piece of pie. Looking at the woman, holding her.

"Your friend goin to Canada, Patrik," Connors said, turning his head, looking across the dark room towards the cage. "Ain't nothing out there that can stop him now." And then, when Patrik didn't answer, his voice lowering, "Worryin don't help it. Don't make sense to worry, Patrik."

Well, they would all find out about it soon enough. Because one week later, to the day, George would be brought back. His story preceded him in bits and pieces, and it was quite a story so that everyone was telling and retelling it, trying to get it straight.

It seemed that the two had made it all the way to the woman's place undetected and without injury, a trip which took at least two days — maybe more, no one could be sure as it was in another county, northwest of the prison.

The woman lived with her son, a boy of about twelve. Also in the house was an old aunt whom the woman took care of and who, according to sketchy reports received from the guards, almost had to be murdered to keep her mouth shut.

One of the jobs the boy had been given was to burn the prisoners' clothes although these could not possible be their original ones, the rural South being far too generous with changes of wardrobe hanging on clotheslines even in winter, left out all night to dry, or maybe to dampen — who knows? — for ironing in the morning.

The boy however did not burn the clothes. If dogs would be used, the scent would end right at their door. Why not detour the dogs, trail the clothes off into the woods?

So this is exactly what he did, tying both sets of clothes by a long rope to the back of his bicycle, dragging them down the road and into the trees, and then, still not content, continuing with them into the woods and leaving them under a pile of leaves.

The excellence of this plan proved futile, however, due only to George's perpetual bad luck. Anyone else might easily have been saved by it.

Meanwhile the woman had designed a plan of her own. She would drive the men in her own car, one by one, to the next state. They would wear wigs and dresses, like it or not, and to hell with retrieving the Canadian's truck. For all they knew it was being watched. Also, the roadside saloon where the truck was parked was south; freedom, if they could get there fast enough, was north.

Although the woman had some men's pants, great baggy coveralls on the pantry hook, she insisted her friend use the old lady's clothes, selecting a large coat, a scarf and a hat to further disguise him, all of this to no avail — the Canadian's bulk being much too round, his legs too thick, and his skin too coarse. And on top of it all, no wig could hide that the hair on his head, on the backs of his hands and the front of his legs, was a long and wiry flaming red.

When they finally left he went as a man, still arguing as they went out the door, his position being if she would only take him to his truck, he could outrun the sheriff all the way to Canada.

So George and the boy were left alone. For a few minutes after the car pulled out, they listened. Then, satisfied that it would not return, the boy got up, went to the fridge and took out a beer for each of them. He sat back down at the table across from George and slid him a beer.

Finally, George spoke. "You think she's going to take him to his truck?"

The boy shook his head. "Nope."

"He gave me his key." George put the key on the table. "So I could get it for him, if she didn't."

"And take it where?"

"Train station up in Charlotte. Said to just leave it there."

The boy looked up at George. "Maybe you stole the key from him."

"Maybe." George sighed. "Either way, he needs his truck. How else can he get it?"

For a few seconds the boy looked steadily at George. "So what is it? You want me to go for it?"

"You know where it is?"

The boy picked up the key, turning it over in his hand. "I've seen the place," he said quietly.

"Maybe you could just go by, check if it's there."

"I'm supposed to stay here, take care of … " he looked over his shoulder, indicating the old aunt's bedroom.

"I know." George looked down at the table. He paused. "Tell you what," he looked back at the boy. "Draw me a map. Can you do that?"

For a few moments the boy didn't answer. "They'll kill you," he said finally, "if you go down there." He was looking away, towards the window.

He got up quickly then, putting the key in his pocket. "I might as well ride over there on my bike — take a look." He crossed the room to the door, took his jacket from a hook and put it on. "It's a long ride. If they come for you while I'm gone, you could jump into that mud-hole back of the house. You might be okay. They might follow the other scent."

George stood. He didn't know what to do he was so grateful to this little kid. "Might not make sense to drive it. Don't drive it — okay?"

"Why not?" The boy grinned. He tightened the belt on his jacket. "Shit. I'm twelve years old. I've been drivin trucks like that old Ford for years."

Well, George must have spent the next few hours trying on different sets of lady's clothes, and being skinny he must have found quite a few that fit. He probably chose the longest though, because of his height, no matter that it was ragged and out of date, because it was this same black cotton skirt with big buttons all the way down the front that he was still wearing when they brought him back, although you could hardly tell what it was — ripped and caked with blood, and stuck together against his legs. And you might have thought that in all that time someone would have had the decency to give him a pair of pants.

It's safe to assume that George would want nothing to do with the old aunt. He'd never wake her intentionally, and when she did wake up, when the sheriff and his dogs were in the yard, he would need to think fast how to handle her. He had found a wrench on the back porch but if he showed it to her, tried to threaten her, she'd scream. Should he warn her calmly to be quiet, not to bust him or … or what? Of course she'd bust him. His only hope was that when she opened that door she'd look so old and crazy, standing there in her nightdress without a tooth in her mouth, that neither man nor dog would know what to believe.

So with just the wrench and a prayer he was through the kitchen, out the back and down the steps, full speed ahead just as the sheriff knocked on the door, running with that long black skirt hiked up and everything under it flopping away, leaping with his brown bony legs over all the various things that clutter up a yard, and then continuing down the hill to the edge of the mud-hole the boy had advised.

It's a sure bet he didn't want to get into that mud. He must have waited until the last possible moment when the dogs were onto his scent with a fury, barking and yapping and raising hell, racing around the side of the house with all of the sheriff's men behind them. He must have waited 'til he could almost see them.

Now the mud-hole wasn't all mud. It was muddy water on top and watery mud on the bottom. It was just deep enough to get into, a greenish swampy pool about which even a frog might have some doubts.

There were plenty of reeds though, around the darker edges of the hole, as well as floating bark and other debris so that if a person could slide under, legs first, walking forward on his elbows until he was completely submerged, he might not be noticed from up above.

Well, he had to do it. Another thing he had to do was keep breathing. Like countless other American kids, George had seen this accomplished in films by breaking off a long reed and breathing through the hollow stem. Like most of us, however, he had never actually tried it. Not only can these reeds be slippery, resilient, and difficult to break, it must be the old brown ones that are hollow because the young green ones are no help at all, and the yellowish green ones aren't much better. George's reed was a yellowish brown.

So there he was, with his heart pumping wildly, completely submerged in the mud and the darkness, trying to suck a little bit of air through that skinny little tube.

And of course he had to worry about bullets. Maybe the men would start firing at random, shoot up the whole pool!

But most of all he had to worry about the one — the single particular dog that was closer than all the rest, jumping into the mud and out again, not only sure that George was in there but sure of exactly *where* he was in there — insisting on it!

'He's probably wagging his tail,' George thought, 'he's so damn happy about finding me.'

He could have come into the water — this one that was insisting. It was slimy but he could have managed it. Instead, he ran up and down, up and down, looking for something to climb out on.

He decided upon a fallen tree branch, walking out on it as far as he could. From here he could actually see George, peering down to confirm his suspicions while the branch sagged beneath his weight.

And all of this occurring while George lay still as death on the bottom of the pond, his single reed sitting stupidly above him just asking to be shot at.

He prayed — prayed that the dog would capsize the branch, fall into the water. He prayed that the men hadn't noticed him yet — that something, anything, would distract them.

And then it did. It did! The dogs were being called ... retreating. George inched backwards, using his elbows. He heard some whistles, some shouts. Then, suddenly, it was quiet. No dogs. No shouting. Nothing. Not a damn thing.

But the one ... the *one* was still there. No matter that he was alone, no matter that the other dogs were gone. *This* dog wasn't going anywhere. He was waiting. He knew.

So it was just George and the dog. That's all it was.

George came up carefully, looking around. The dog was still on the branch, panting happily, tongue hanging out of the side of his mouth. He couldn't have been more than three feet away. Incredibly, he looked like he was grinning.

George did his best to sit up casually, as if nothing were wrong, as if he hardly noticed the dog was there. The dog trembled; he let out a little yelp, a little growl. He quivered. The hair on his back stood straight up. He began to lift each paw carefully and put it down again, making the tree branch sway and dip slowly ... to the left ... to the right ... to the left.

George moved, just slightly. The dog lowered his head and growled a low gravely growl; his ears went back, up, and back again. George stopped. So did the dog.

George gathered his legs beneath him, preparing to stand. He came up a few inches, holding the wrench under the water. He stared at the dog; dogs were supposed to cower when a man did that. George waited. Here, obviously, was a dog who didn't know the rules.

'As soon as he blinks' George was thinking, 'the minute that he blinks ...'

But the dog didn't blink.

And it wasn't a he. *She* didn't blink.

It was the kind of stand off in which neither party can possibly win. Its resolution occurs somewhere else. The best we can do is be prepared for it or, in some cases, maintain our dignity while we try to catch up with it.

George hesitated. So did she. She gave him a quick, questioning kind of look. And then she just lay down, put her head on her paws, and closed her eyes.

So he could grab her? ... pull her under? George studied the dog. He should kill her quickly, before anyone missed her. He got ready to do it. He took a breath. And then he stopped.

He couldn't do it. No decent human being could do it.

But reality was present also, swinging around with a vengeance. And in the next instant the dog had leapt to her feet, jumped onto the bank, and was raising so much hell that five more dogs were racing down the hill to join her, surprising George so much that he slipped, fell into the mud and dropped the wrench.

And then, right there, he put it all together. He knew that the truck was never coming, that the boy had long ago been caught, and that the entire episode with the dog had been staged.

But she had saved him by what she had done because the men who were watching — hiding and waiting for him to pull her under, to raise that wrench, would have shot him the moment that he did.

So that George, realizing all of this, and willing to give credit where credit was due, struggled to his feet, raised both his arms, and surrendered.

Now that was what really happened. Most people, however, had other versions. The most popular version, and you can see the temptation to believe this, was that George was found in bed — in *bed* with the white woman. So deep a vicarious pleasure did the men in Bunkhouse One seem to take from this version, that George was becoming a kind of hero to them, and Patrik, not having the heart to discourage them, kept his thoughts to himself.

It took three days from the day they heard that George was caught, until they saw him, until he was returned to the camp. And every night Patrik would sit alone in the cage and listen to the stories of other black men whom white women had favored. 'It's just the racial thing,' he'd tell himself. 'It's how it used to be. Forget it.'

But he couldn't. And as the nights wore on with their jokes, their vulgarities, a creeping sense of isolation came into the cage, and Patrik began to understand how alone he was. And he remembered Calvin. And he remembered Lowe.

'My God,' he thought, 'George is my friend. I never should have let him go alone.'

Until the day they had been waiting for arrived. They came in from work to hear that George was back. Thank Heaven. He hadn't been killed or shipped off somewhere else. And Patrik felt a great wave of relief, a great surge of happiness. He even allowed himself the luxury of a few comments about old George, even accepted a few compliments.

Because it was true. Woman or no woman, George had given the sheriff one hell of a chase and he'd survived it all. And Patrik had to admit that he was really feeling kind of proud of George that night.

Spirits were dampened a bit, however, by the news that they would not be able to see him for a while. Nobody talked much as they ate; everyone watched the door. They saved him some dinner, piling it high with contributions from their own plates. They paced around, rolled cigarettes.

Then, about 9 p.m., the door opened. The warden entered first, followed by a tall sinewy white man whom no one had ever seen before — a pale, deadly looking character dressed as a state trooper, high boots, helmet.

After him, came George. But George wasn't walking; he was being carried by two of the camp guards. Patrik looked at the guards. No, not these two — they weren't the ones who had done this to George.

Because George … had been beaten. He hung now, swaying slightly like an empty hammock between the guards. He looked sunken, caved in. He couldn't be dead — could he?

Damn! Wait a minute. DAMN!

But they were walking fast with him, carrying him straight to the cage, not looking anywhere else, ashamed probably or scared, moving along in a line, military fashion, so no one could really see how badly George was hurt.

When they got to the cage the warden and the state policeman stepped aside, and the two guards went in with George. "Which one is his?" this from one of the guards, "… which cot?" No one answered.

The warden who was holding, along with his shotgun, George's new set of chains, walked into the cage. "Right there," he gestured towards George's bunk, "on top."

Patrik began to move. It can truthfully be said that in that moment he had only the vaguest idea of what he was doing. He understood that he was approaching the cage but he did not yet realize that he had picked up the room's only chair — Taylor's chair, and that he was carrying it as he walked.

"Leave the irons, Warden." Patrik stopped. "Get them out of there. You come out too," he added.

The warden turned. There was no way he could be worried, standing there with his shotgun, but he was cautious. He looked down the cage towards the two guards. They were heaving George as smoothly as possible onto his bunk, rolling him so that his back was to them all.

For a moment they waited, looking out at Patrik. So deathly quiet was the room, that when after a few seconds George grunted, moving slightly in an attempt to pull his knees up to his chest, the sound went through the room like an electric shock.

"Come out now," Patrik was still holding the chair. It was an odd sight because although he was talking to the men in the cage, his energy was focused on the stranger outside of it. So intent was Patrik upon preventing this man from entering the cage, he looked like an animal trainer faced with a beast who might go berserk.

"Hurry up," he said to the warden, as if the animal might spring.

The warden let the chains slide from his hand; they clattered on the floor of the cage. "Put them on him later, Taylor," he said and he turned abruptly, came out of the cage, and began walking in his normal business-like manner towards the door. He ignored Patrik. Patrik let him pass.

Next, the guards. They also passed. But the stranger, the moment that he moved, was blocked.

"I'm not the one who did this to your friend." His voice was harsh; it cracked abrasively in the silent room. And yet, the pitch was off; it seemed high, too high for a man of his appearance. It seemed offensive, tremendously offensive.

"No?" Patrik was trembling. "Maybe not." He was feeling extremely strange now; the face before him stood out like an apparition, as if it were disembodied. The pupils were shrinking before his eyes and he noticed the lines within the iris elongate, as if someone were drawing them.

"What are you doing here?" he said quietly.

But it was fading now — the face, the apparition, replaced by an emptiness that was even worse, a terrible uncertainty, a vacuum.

'What's happening to me?' he was thinking, trying desperately to pull back, to feel the present, the reality of his body, his surroundings, to feel the safety of them.

But he couldn't. And when Smith came up behind him and touched him the touch seemed startling, and again — visibly, even to himself, he trembled.

'I'm all right,' he was thinking. 'All I have to do is put down the chair. I'm holding this chair and it's got everybody worried.'

He put the chair down carefully. He felt Connors beside him then, on the other side.

"Connors," he said. "What am I doing?"

"You ain't done nothin," Connors took his arm. "You need to sit down, Patrik. See the table? Look here at the table where we always sit."

Patrik was shaking. He looked at the table. Slowly he sat down on its long bench. He looked at the floor.

"Let him go now," Connors was saying. "Whoever you saw let him go."

So gradually he did. Someone brought him a rag and he wiped his face, and when he looked up again the stranger was gone, and George lay on his bunk alone.

So that's how Murdok got into the bunkhouse. It was the only way he could get in. But he never got in again.

Well, they did everything they could for poor George, taking him out of the cage, making a mattress for him on the floor. Taylor heated water and Miller lit a small lamp, placing it next to George, and together they bathed his face, his eyes, his ears.

The other men scrubbed down in the courtyard while this was going on, quietly joining Taylor, sitting on the floor beside George. And then carefully, minutely, they undressed him, and examined his whole body, and washed all of his wounds. And there were parts of him so badly bruised they could not bear to touch them, and over these parts they poured water gently.

So the night wore on, and their work — painstakingly slow, continued. Once, as Taylor lifted George's head to help him drink he had to pull the cup away, the water had turned so red with blood.

And as he was washing the part of him that made him a man — would have made him a man, if he'd ever really had the chance, if he had not been cut so cruelly, cut down in his youth, in his beauty ... down from the cross, limp and pale, no mother, no sister to comfort him here ... while this washing was taking place Taylor began to moan. "When your father and mother desert you," he prayed, "then the Lord will take you up."

And when they had finished and had covered him, this moaning became the moaning of many; it became a chant and a prayer that filled the room. And to Patrik it was an overwhelming thing to see this group of tough old men praying over George like this, each reciting his own verse, his own scripture.

Once towards morning when the room was quiet, Patrik felt George reach up and touch his face. He looked down and saw that George's eyes were open, just a fraction.

George motioned for Patrik to come closer. His voice was dry in Patrik's ear and his breath smelled like blood. "I lost three teeth," he said simply.

Patrik nodded.

"There was an old lady. That's why they did this — going to put a rape charge on me."

"Never mind. It won't stick. We'll get you out of here before that."

"When?"

"Soon. Just rest. As soon as you're well."

And Patrik looked down at the broken, battered body of his friend. And he turned his face away. And for the last time in his life — this is true — he wept.

CHAPTER XIV

So it was to be a long winter — long for Patrik who worked alone, whose questions stopped, whose grief turned inward, and long for George who lived only in the cage now, who laid on his cot month after month, all day, all night, dreaming quietly in his little space.

It must have looked too easy. Because as the months moved along slowly with very little to report, those in authority began to discuss, between poker games and steaks, between church meetings and wife beatings, what they could do to punish further an "incorrigible" like George.

The reason George was considered incorrigible was that during this time, in spite of his condition, he made six more attempts to escape. These were not serious attempts. No one was threatened or hurt, no weapons used.

Nevertheless, at least four of these incidents were considered "attempts." What he would do, since he could not run, was walk — simply walk away whenever he saw the opportunity. From the hospital, for example, because by the end of the first week he was coughing up so much blood that Taylor went personally to the warden about it. Then, two weeks after that, from the warden's office itself.

The warden had decided to take another look at him because according to Taylor, although the bleeding had stopped, the coughing hadn't. And to top it all off, George was still losing weight. George waited patiently until the warden turned his back to answer the telephone. Then he simply walked out of the office, down the steps and out the gate.

He never resisted when they caught him on these occasions. He never started running or tried to hide. He just walked until they stopped him.

Although several of George's ribs had been broken and although one of these ribs must have punctured a lung, his healing was further complicated by what appeared to be either pneumonia or pleurisy, or a combination of the two. In fact, it was Taylor who made this diagnosis, and it was Taylor who smuggled in some penicillin and gave it to George every day until it ran out, probably saving his life.

Another three attempts were made with a new prisoner named Joey. Joey was an expert mechanic who could start, in ten seconds or less, any vehicle left unattended in the camp yard, at the camp gate, or on the camp road. George, sensing the opportunity, would just casually follow Joey as far as he could — walking, of course. It was an admirable effort but that's all it was. No one expected Joey to wait. All things considered, the warden decided to let two of these incidents slide.

Although Joey was recaptured, beaten, and charged for each of his escapes, George was no longer beaten. He was considered too sick to beat. There wasn't any way to hurt him without the serious risk of killing him.

Once when Coats was bringing in his crew from work, he came right up alongside of George who, incredibly, was strolling along the camp road. Coats stopped the truck and George got into the back.

"What was that about?" Patrik had asked him.

After a few seconds George shrugged. "Just doing my part," he said simply.

Joey finally made it on his fourth attempt and George was left alone again, all day, every day.

Sometime around the middle of March, George began to read. Occasionally the men would have magazines sent to them and George had clipped a coupon sending for a free book, *The Mastery of Life*. George began to read this book. He stopped trying to walk away. He simply read, and slept, and laid there. And no one bothered him anymore.

The warden must have pondered a long time about George. He consulted Taylor. In early April he must have decided that George was going to die. He applied to have him transferred to the state penitentiary.

It was the end of April, a Sunday. The cage was open.

"What's happening, George?" Patrik looked up.

"Not much." George sat down across the table from him.

"I'm filing a complaint," Patrik looked down at the papers in front of him, "to Washington, D.C."

George smiled slowly. He looked like someone who was very sleepy.

"Good. That's good, Patrik."

"I figured ... can't hurt to try."

George continued to smile. He nodded. He was terribly thin, thinner than Patrik had ever seen him.

"You know, there are some exercises you could do — sit-ups, that kind of thing."

George didn't answer.

"Well ... you know, when you're ready." Patrik looked up again. George was looking directly at him. He had the clearest eyes, intelligent, gentle. They were beautiful eyes actually. "You're feeling better, eh?"

"I've been right here all along," George looked back at him. "What happened? You forgot?"

"Shit," Patrik turned away, "I thought you were trying to die on me, man, you laid on that cot so long."

For a few seconds George was silent. "You know, that's a strange thing about you, Patrik. Whenever you go away in your mind from someone and then come back, you always think it was the other person who moved."

Patrik looked down again at the letter he had been trying to write. He let out a long breath. "Maybe ... sometimes ... we all do it, George. You too."

But he hadn't moved far. And neither had George. Sometimes we can't. We'd like to move farther, never come back, forget all the headaches that drag us down, confuse us, sap the very life from us. But ... we just can't.

And Patrik thought about Robin, making her way down the streets of Miami, passing the spot where Lowe had died, where he staggered ... where he fell, trying to ignore it, strutting along.

Even the little ones, Violet and Jason, saving their pennies, doing their homework, they had the same thing to deal with: the terrible caring behind it all, the wordless sorrow, the inevitable knowledge that it doesn't matter much what we do, how hard we try ... or don't try, we're all going down in the end. We're all going back to God.

Patrik had been six years old when he had seen death for the first time. He had been walking home with Nathan. Someone had been shot; a crowd was gathering.

It had been a young man, about seventeen, dark-skinned. The single officer on the scene had been young too, no more than twenty — fair skin, grey eyes. He hadn't been the one to kill the boy but he had been the first to find him.

He had been so nervous, down on one knee, feeling for the boy's pulse, listening for his breath, the crowd pressing in on him closer and closer.

He had noticed Patrik then, stopped what he was doing and looked right at him. And Patrik saw the shame and the outrage in his eyes, and he realized that the cop had been trying — right at that moment, to place the blame for this death, to separate from it, to pull his soul back.

But he couldn't.

And Patrik saw that there were tears in the cop's eyes, tears in the eyes of a white cop. But no one was white in Miami that night. And no one was black. And everyone's brother, and everyone's child, lay dead on the street.

The letters Patrik had been writing bore fruit in May. Two men from the Justice Department appeared at the camp in suits and ties, ostensibly to interview prisoners, make personal observations, and file a report. They did not however interview any prisoners.

According to George they came in, looked around, and left. Possibly, they tried to talk to him. But the way George would see it — what was the point? Prisons exist to punish people. Abuse has always been part of the plan.

But George should have tried. He was sixteen and he was dying. It wouldn't have hurt to try.

"It's for me, you know." It was a few weeks later. Patrik had just come in from work. George continued, "That tomb they're building in the yard. Did you see it?"

"I saw it. It might not be for you."

"Who's it for, then?"

"I don't know — could be for anything. Storage. Something like that."

"Patrik, they've got blueprints. Federal Government sent them blueprints, came in here and sized me up."

Patrik washed his hands and face, walked back to the bunk and sat down on his cot.

"Why? What have you done? You ain't done nothin for a long time, George."

George didn't answer.

"Forget about it." Patrik stretched out on his cot. "They haven't got a reason in the world to put you in that ... whatever it is."

Patrik woke up around midnight. It had rained and the air was damp. He thought about the strange box-like structure being built in the yard — concrete block. In the summer it would be suffocating in there ... no light ... no air.

"George?"

"Yeah."

"I've been thinking. Maybe you're right. Why else would they be building it?"

"See what I mean?"

"But why? To hide you?"

"I don't even care, Patrik. They might as well put me in it."

For a few minutes Patrik lay still. He sat up then looking through the bars across the dark room. He listened. Taylor was asleep.

"It's time to go, George," he said quietly. "Do you hear what I'm saying?" He paused, waiting for George to answer. "Can you make it to the highway? That's all you have to do — make it to the highway. Can you do that?"

But the cage was still.

"What have you got to lose, George?"

"It's not that. I know I don't have anything to lose."

"Then what?"

"Ain't got nowhere to go."

Patrik swallowed. "Sure we do. We'll find somewhere."

"Where? New York?"

"It doesn't have to be New York. Someplace else."

For a long time the room was quiet.

"Forget it Patrik," George said finally. "I'm sick. Let me sleep."

But Patrik was awake now, fully awake. 'I'm going to get him out of here' he said quietly, to himself — to God. 'Watch. This time I'll do it right.'

The usual means of transportation used by camp prisoners (some of the men made little trips on the weekend, conjugal visits you might say,) was by bicycle. "There's plenty of rusty old bikes all over them woods," Smith had told them after their first attempt. "I'm surprised you boys didn't fall over 'em."

"So, how close do you think those bicycles are?" Patrik had asked Smith the night after his conversation with George. "Can two of them be moved up — hidden up the hill, next to the camp road?"

"Well, that can be done," Smith answered, "but I think you should know, I think you should consider," they were sitting on Smith's cot, "that the problem with George isn't just physical. He can walk just fine. That isn't it."

But Patrik wasn't listening. This time — this time — he was going to do it right.

"Taylor, where's George?" It was one week later. Patrik had come in from work to find the cage empty.

"Don't know. I'm trying to find him myself." Taylor was unlocking the courtyard gate. "You look in here. I'll check the office."

"Taylor, hold on." Patrik walked over to Taylor and touched his shoulder. "If he's not there, at the office, don't say anything. Don't ask for him. Follow me?"

Taylor turned, his hand on the gate. "So they can kill him? Is that what you want?"

"Maybe he got away, walked away."

"We'd know about it. Guards would know."

"Maybe not. Maybe no one saw him."

Taylor looked as though he were considering the possibility. He sighed. "Patrik, I'm trustee. George is missing and you expect me to say nothing?"

"Yes. I expect you to give him a chance. One chance."

Taylor looked past Patrik at the empty cage. "Fix up his bed, then." And he walked away.

So for the next few hours no one said a thing about it. Patrik dummied up the cot and they all had supper as usual. Finally, just before lights out, Patrik walked over to Connors and sat down on the floor beside his cot.

"Connors," he spoke quietly, "tell me, what do you honestly think?"

"Patrik, listen here now." Connors, who had been rolling a few pieces of tobacco into an inch of brown paper, leaned forward and lit the tiny piece of cigarette. He took a short smoke, then passed it to Patrik,

"I hope he got away, just like you do. But it don't seem likely. From what we can find out, they took him out of here today. He's in the box."

Patrik looked away, "He can't be; it's not finished."

"They finished it today."

Patrik looked down at the floor. He pressed out the half inch of paper. "Well, he can't make it. He'll die in there, Connors. He's too sick."

"He might not die. George is tougher than most people think."

"How long do you think he's got?"

"Depends on how hot it gets, where his mind is at. Some men go crazy quick. Without enough water, he could die in a week. Others ..."

Patrik waited. "Others what?"

"Well, I heard of a case where a man did a month in a box like that. Four weeks and three days, and he walked out. Rationed his water. Did exercises in there. Kept track of things — didn't let his mind slip."

"He won't do it, Connors. You know how he is." Patrik bowed his head. "He won't exercise; he won't do any of it."

"He will if he has a reason. We can get him out of here, Patrik, just like you want. We can set it up. But you have to help him too."

"I'll help him. I'll carry him if I have to."

"That's not what I mean. You have to help him now. Talk to him. You have to talk to him, Patrik."

For a long second Patrik looked at Connors. "They'd never do it — put me in there with him. Never."

"Sure they would. There's two compartments in there, side by side. Warden probably ordered it like that."

"And if he won't put me in it?"

"Ask him to."

The next day Patrik refused to go to work. He demanded to see the warden. By now, everyone in the camp knew that George was in the box. The guards, one by one, came into the bunkhouse, saw the dummy, and laughed. They pushed Patrik roughly back into the cage and slammed it shut.

Then everybody left for work.

Patrik waited. At nine a.m. he was taken out and hung on the fence. "The warden's busy," he was told. Next day, same thing.

The morning of the third day, Coats himself came into the cage. He looked at Patrik. "I want you to work. You coming to work?"

"I have to see the warden first."

"And then?"

"And then I'll work."

The warden saw him that morning.

"Where's George?"

"George is being transferred to the state penitentiary. Until then, he's being secured."

"Where is he?"

"He's under strict security."

"You killed him, didn't you?"

"You know where he is, Patrik. Everyone in this camp knows

where he is." The warden looked at Patrik suspiciously. "And don't try to bargain with me. I'm not going to put you in there with him. You're needed to work."

"I want to see if he's still alive."

"No."

"Do you want him to die in there?"

"He won't die."

"Yes he will."

For a moment the warden seemed to hesitate. "If you go in there with him, you can't come out. You stay as long as he does. Until the day he's transferred."

"Good. Fine. Perfect."

The warden studied Patrik carefully. "Why do you want to do this?"

"Because it's my fault he's here. He didn't steal the whiskey; I did."

"And?"

"And because he's my friend."

CHAPTER XV

Hotboxes have been around for a long time. By most accounts they've co-existed with prison farms and labor camps across the South for as long as there's been someone to put in them. Designs vary but the idea is the same. Heat from the sun penetrates the box, often assisted by aluminum siding, (a discarded cast iron furnace was once considered an appropriate hotbox,) and cannot escape. Of course, the box is versatile. Prisoners can suffocate or go mad even without the heat.

The structure within which Patrik and George were confined, however, went a step beyond the normal punitive design. This hotbox came equipped with a heating unit of its own, a man-made heater. You heard me — in a hotbox.

The box had almost no outside ventilation. An enclosed concrete structure with less than one inch of air space at floor level, it stood just over four feet high and had one door. Two cells, 3'x 5' each, faced this door next to which stood the heater, reminding the guard who came each morning with bread and water to fire it up before he left. This, he assumed, was his job. Obviously, the heater was there to be used. No one was trying to kill these boys but a hotbox should stay hot. Wasn't that the point? To be completely fair to the camp guards, maybe it was. If the hotbox came with a set of instructions, nobody read them.

The cells, of course, were unfurnished. In the middle of each was a circular drain about six inches in diameter, and in the corner was a bucket. The bucket was to be handed out daily to one of the guards whose job was to dump it, add new water (under half a bucket, usually about a third,) a splash of disinfectant, and return it. Luckily, most of the guards were too lazy to add the disinfectant so the water was safe enough to drink as well as to use liberally on the skin, (although the word liberal here is a joke because if the guards forgot them, which they often did, they would have to stretch this water for another day.

Actually, there was hardly any use for the disinfectant. Bowels move only when they have been able to accumulate some waste. This means, on a very meager diet, about once a week.

It was a mixed blessing however, being forgotten by the morning guard, because although there would be no water that day, no food, no burst of light when the door opened, thankfully there would be no heater either.

The guard who came at night was more dependable. But he only came to turn off the heater and see if they were still alive. Messages from Bunkhouse One were rare. Some biscuits, a few aspirin, a brief word of encouragement — that was about all they could expect. But it helped.

During the day they lay on the floor, faces on the concrete where it was at least a little cooler. Once the heater was turned off, however, and the heat dissipated, the temperature would drop into the low fifties, and they would sit up shivering in their sweat-soaked clothes.

They started exercising simply to keep warm, doing sit-ups, counting them. There was no routine to it but without the heater at least they had some energy. And it was quieter; they could talk.

Sometimes they talked on and off all night. They knew that once this practice was established, it could save them only if they held to it. So they did. For six weeks, they held on fast. They didn't let the lifeline slip.

Because just as Patrik had been willing to put his life on hold for George, George must have decided to put his death on hold for Patrik. He could not allow himself to rot away, his body stinking in that little suffocating box next to his friend. He must have thought about it and decided he just couldn't do that to Patrik. He would have to die later.

Also, he now had something to look forward to — the impending transfer. Patrik had told him about the escape plan but he didn't take that seriously. He pretended that he did for Patrik's sake, and he discussed it for the companionship of discussing it, but that was all. Even as he listened to the details, the bicycles and disguises hidden in the brush, the route they would take to avoid the sheriff, he did it mainly as a mental exercise.

Some nights they would break down their journey by miles, back through Columbia, down through the long state and over the line to Augusta. Once safely in Georgia, however, they would begin to delight in the trip, and they would estimate the distances between houses and barns, places where they could find water and food, the little burnt out shacks where they could rest.

On this mental journey they had no help, no money, no truck to carry them through the night. All they had were the bikes.

But the bikes were their wings. With the bikes they could fly.

The perfect route, they decided one night, would be to avoid Columbia and take #302 directly south. No one would look for them on #302. No one was ever on #302. Some nights they became so involved in this fantasy that they would doze off and dream about it. And they would visualize themselves coming down through the dark hills of Aiken County, approaching the fork in the road, the white grocery store, pedaling just like maniacs, right through the town while the sheriff slept.

But it was Route #1 into Augusta, down-hill all the way, that they loved the best. Ahh ... and they would imagine how it would feel, flying along on their bicycles in ladies' skirts with scarves around their heads, skimming along that empty road, down the last mile to the state line, legs straight out, pedals spinning by themselves.

And if one of them fell, hit a rock or a ditch, grabbing the bike and getting back on, not even minding — laughing about it, yelling at each other in the black wind, flying along like angels, or better yet like witches, riding on their broomsticks out of hell.

On several occasions George tried to tell Patrik that, in spite of the excellence of this plan, it might be better just to scrap it. He would really rather go to the state penitentiary. In fact he had been hoping for a transfer all along. With two successful and four unsuccessful attempts to escape, he felt he had earned it. Also he was sick. He couldn't work. And this was a work camp.

Now although all of this made perfect sense, even to Patrik, the reason — the *reason* — George wanted the transfer made no sense at all. Somehow he believed that he was going to get an "office job."

"A what?"

"You know, filing reports, that kind of thing. I could learn to type, educate myself. Maybe I could start drawing again. They'd have plenty of paper, pencils; a big place like that has everything, Patrik."

"George. Think for a minute. You're talking about a maximum-security prison. What they have is murderers, men who haven't seen a girl for twenty years. What about that?"

"F you, Patrik. I wouldn't be around that type of prisoner. Don't you listen to an F-ing thing?"

"Okay. Then tell me this. Why would they give you an office job? If they have such a thing, wouldn't it be for prisoners who have skills already? Wouldn't it be for people who were lawyers or judges before they were busted?"

"Judges?"

"Yeah. Bank clerks or … I don't know, insurance salesman."

But George persisted. He was sure, he was convinced that he could get an office job.

So they just dropped it finally in order to keep peace.

And they continued to plan their trip, down the long hill to Augusta, in their witches' costumes, on their bicycles, out of hell.

They were released from the hotbox at 5 p.m., the night before the transfer. Two of the camp guards helped them into the bunkhouse, gave them a new set of clothes and waited while they took a shower. This, however, was not the end of it. They stayed. The guards stayed in the bunkhouse.

At first they made themselves busy, bringing food and coffee to the cage, offering cigarettes and, in general, complimenting the boys on how well they had held up. It was too damn long, they agreed, for anyone to spend in a hotbox.

It was the strangest thing observing these guards. Did they plan to stay all night? At any rate, the boys were grateful for the chance to stretch out; they lay down on their cots and rested.

About half an hour after lights out, Patrik opened his eyes. The guards were still there. He could hear Taylor snoring. He closed his eyes.

It must have been close to eleven when he woke up with a start. Someone had reached through the side of the cage and nudged him. He sat straight up. The guards, together with Smith and Connors, were going out the door of the bunkhouse. Patrik waited. Carefully he worked his irons up around his calves. After a few seconds he got up.

George was sitting on his cot, watching the door. Patrik motioned to him: *let's go.*

They moved quietly to the end of the cage, opened it and stepped down into the room. No one stirred. Taylor was still snoring. Incredibly, the guards had left their shotguns propped up against the outside of the cage. George hesitated, looking at the guns: *should we?* Patrik followed his gaze: *hell, no.*

Patrik and George crossed the room. They slipped out into the yard and stood for a moment looking around. There was a new spotlight over the gate but otherwise nothing had changed.

They began to make their way to the gate, staying in the dark as much as possible. It was locked.

"We've got to go over." Patrik looked at his friend. "Can you make it?" George didn't answer. "Stand on my shoulders."

It was right at that moment that someone — another prisoner, came out of the darkness and grabbed Patrik by the arm. "This way," he said, "around to the back."

Patrik and George followed. He wasn't the only prisoner out there. The door to Bunkhouse Two, at the far end of the yard, was open. Several men were ahead of them, disappearing around the edge of the building. The single bulb, strung up on a pole behind Bunkhouse Two, was dark. The men had dug under the fence right at that point and now the first of these (or maybe not the first, there was no way to tell,) was down on his side, pushing under. He made it. The next. Another. A line began to form. Patrik looked around nervously. No guards. No trustees. Damn!

The remaining men were crouched down along the fence, waiting their turn. Patrik and George moved up behind them. Briefly, they looked back. No one from Bunkhouse One had followed. Smith and Connors were nowhere to be seen; they had taken the guards the other way. Patrik smiled inwardly. This, then, was to be a "white" escape.

The prisoner in front of Patrik was getting ready to go, only one man before him. Patrik moved up beside him. "Do you know if there's any help for us out there? Any transportation?"

The prisoner turned as if surprised.

"You George?"

"No. That's George — right there."

The white prisoner strained to see George. He looked back at Patrik. "There's a tractor trailer on the highway. Georgia tags. He'll take anyone who makes it. You coming too?"

Patrik nodded.

"Okay," he was down very low. "Good luck." And he was under.

Patrik followed. He pulled himself up on the other side and turned. George was inching under the wire. Patrik looked through the fence. Someone was running across the yard towards them — *damn!*

Patrik looked down. George was having trouble. He reached to help him. He looked up again, through the fence.

Good God, it was Taylor — Taylor with something under one of his arms, waving the other one, coming right at them.

George, who was about half way through, rolled onto his hip and looked back. Taylor made a dive for his leg and caught it. George grabbed the fence from the outside and held steady. For a moment neither he nor Taylor moved.

While this was happening, the prisoner who had gone before Patrik reappeared. "Watch out," he said quietly, and he threw something across the ground to George. George caught it. It was a knife. "Use it," he said. He looked at Patrik, "Tell him to use it." He began moving backwards. "There's a lot of us, man. Don't let that gun go off."

What gun? Patrik watched George. He was pushing back under now, holding the knife. It was impossible to see if Taylor had a gun.

Yeah. Sure. After they left him two of them propped up against the cage.

"Let me go, Taylor," George was out of breath. They were

struggling. Suddenly George freed himself, stood, and pulled Taylor to his feet.

"What's this?" He took the gun. "Why do you have this? You want to kill me?" He looked through the fence at Patrik. "How do you like this shit?"

Patrik went back under the fence. He took the shotgun away from George and aimed it at Taylor. "Don't move, Taylor. Go on, George," he indicated the fence. "I'll handle it."

"What are you going to do?"

"Just go. Hurry up."

"Hell, no." George shook his head. "No way, Patrik."

"You sit down," Patrik was prodding Taylor with the gun, "over there ... sit down right there."

Taylor sat down. Patrik turned towards George, "Find something to tie him up."

George looked from Patrik to Taylor. "The both of you are assholes — I can't believe this shit." He walked over to Taylor and crouched down beside him. "Look here, Taylor, give us some time. How much time can you give us? Can you give us twenty minutes?"

Taylor looked at George. He leaned back on his elbows. "I'm a trustee," he said. "I'm responsible for you." He paused, breathing deeply. "I'll give you five."

Suddenly George laughed. He looked at Taylor, let out a long sigh, and then looked back at Patrik. "Go on, Patrik. To hell with it. You go. Let me just sit here for awhile, with my old friend."

"You don't want to go? Really?"

"Really. I really don't." George sat down slowly next to Taylor. "It just ain't worth it, Brother."

Patrik lowered the shotgun. "I don't know what to think about you, George."

"Yeah you do. We're no good at this, Patrik — never were. Let someone else die in the woods out there. I'm tired of it."

Patrik sat down. He sighed. "You'll die in the state penitentiary, then. That's where you'll die."

George leaned back, looking up at the sky. "Think so?"

For a moment they were silent. When George spoke again he was looking at Taylor. "Patrik's got five more years. That's all he got, Taylor. And possibly less that than that, if you don't mention this."

Taylor took a deep breath, looked around the quiet yard, and then looked back at George. "Mention what?" he said.

It seemed like a long time that the three of them sat there before they decided to go in and get some sleep. The yard, the camp, the world was very still.

"Air smells sweet out here," George said finally. And he smiled. "Don't it?"

EPILOGUE

Patrik completed his sentence in April, 1965, his six years reduced to four plus nine months for the first escape. He walked back into Columbia, got a job, a little room in which to stay, and began to save his money. He lived a very quiet life during this time, keeping to himself, making few friends. At night he would take a walk, sit outside on the step to have a cigarette, wash out his work clothes and hang them to dry.

Although he wrote several letters home explaining that he was well and enclosing a few dollars, he never included a return address. He didn't know why he preferred it like this; he just supposed he wasn't ready. So he just worked, and budgeted his money, and saved.

In September, Patrik decided he would get a dog. He devoted an entire Saturday to this, walking across town to the animal shelter, taking his time and choosing carefully. Remembering George's story, he decided upon a female, a mix of German shepherd and collie, a slender gentle creature with smiling eyes and plenty of energy.

Patrik began to take a tremendous amount of pride in this dog, buying her quality dog food and vitamins, taking her out in the early dawn, running with her, and then again each evening — for a longer walk this time, sitting on the floor of his room when they returned, inspecting her ears and paws for burs, brushing her coat until it shone.

He had begun to use the library now, borrowing almost every book allowable on almost every subject that had ever interested him, and he would stay up for hours into the night, alone on his bed while his dog slept peacefully beside him, reading these books. He checked several times for the book that George had been reading in prison but all the copies had been taken out.

If anyone had asked Patrik how he felt that year, as Autumn closed and winter grew across the countryside, he would have answered that he felt extremely well, and that he was, perhaps for the first time in his life, content.

It was Christmas before Patrik decided he would call Lorraine. It had been a year since he had heard from her. She had written last Christmas while he was still in prison, including a picture of her son but mentioning nothing about herself, no details of her personal life. No doubt she was in love with someone else by now and worried that he might come back and interfere.

"Hello, Lorraine. This is Patrik."

"Patrik! I'm so glad you called. Are you all right?"

"Yes, I'm all right. And you?"

"I'm all right too." She paused. "Patrik, I've had no way to reach you."

"I know. Did you get my letters?"

"Yes. And the money. Thank you."

"Never mind; it wasn't much. I … I only have three minutes. I wanted to wish you a happy holiday."

For a moment she was silent. "Would you like to talk to the baby?"

"No … not now." He could hear the child in the background.

"Will you be coming down to see us?"

"I'm not sure. I'm trying to save to buy a car. Maybe then. It would be just for a day or two, when I can get some time off from the job."

"All right." She paused. "I understand."

"I'll let you know. I'll write before I come. Take care. Okay?"

"I will. God bless you, Patrik."

Patrik swallowed. "God bless you too." And he hung up.

Patrik was shaking badly when he left the phone booth. For a long time he lay on his bed that night, staring at the ceiling. Something stirred within him. Her voice.

In April, one year after his release, Patrik bought a car and drove back down to Miami, just for a visit. He did not backtrack on Route One; he took Route 29 directly east, picking up the interstate that ran along the coast.

It was almost seven o'clock in the evening when he arrived at

Lorraine's. Whatever may have happened, he felt he was prepared for it.

It was a tremendous shock though, just seeing her. She came out of the house, the child walking beside her. He couldn't take his eyes from Lorraine. She seemed so beautiful. Had she always been so beautiful?

"Hi," she reached up to kiss him on the cheek. He took her hand, turning his attention to the boy.

"And how are *you?*" He had planned to give the child a hug, then swing him up and put him on his shoulders. But he felt shy now, terrified that the boy would not like him. Finally, he smiled. The boy looked down, then up again; slowly he smiled back.

"Come and see what I've got for you," Patrik moved around to the trunk of his car and opened it. "I've been saving something for you … all this time." It was a glass jar, quart size, filled with pennies, nickels, dimes.

"What's the matter? You don't like it?" — because the boy just stood there looking up at him.

"Tell you what, then. How would you like to meet my dog? Look, she's in the car." Patrik went to the car door and opened it. "Watch out, she's *very* friendly."

Well, the spell was broken for a few minutes because the dog made such a great fuss over everyone they had to laugh, all of them petting her in turn.

"So, how do you like her?"

The boy looked at Patrik. He seemed so … solemn.

"Is something wrong?"

"I'm sorry about your friend. I'm sorry about what happened to him."

Patrik glanced at Lorraine but she was just staring at the boy herself. He looked back at the boy.

"Why? What happened to my friend?"

"He died. Somebody shot him."

Patrik straightened. He glanced over the boy's head towards Calvin's house, then back at Lorraine.

"No," she had followed his glance, "Calvin's fine. He works for the city, helping young people. And he's married. He has a brand new baby girl."

It was the most amazing thing — watching Lorraine. She was standing there smiling at him, telling him all this terrific news about Calvin, and the whole time she was talking her eyes were filling up with tears.

Patrik turned back to the boy. Things were beginning to slip away from him now and he was trying desperately to get a grip on them. He leaned down, closer to the boy.

"What was my friend's name?"

"George Wright."

Patrik leaned back against the car. Lorraine had come over to stand beside him and he looked at her.

"What's this about George? ... Lorraine?"

"I wanted to give you a minute to get settled, before I told you." She looked helplessly at the boy. "We just found out. No one even knew that he was back in town."

"You're saying he was killed here in Miami?"

She nodded.

Patrik looked away. He reached for a cigarette. "That's not possible. George had ten years. He had ten and a half years, Lorraine."

She didn't answer.

"Did you see him? Was there a service for him?"

Lorraine looked down. She shook her head. "No one knew until it was too late. His family's gone. There wasn't anyone to bury him, Patirk."

Patrik moved closer to Lorraine. "It wasn't him. Don't worry. He's in the state penitentiary, Lorraine."

Patrik took a breath. He lowered his voice. "Where did this shooting take place?"

"Up on 36th Street. In one of those trailer parks where only white people live. He was staying with a woman and one day her brother walked in and saw George there and started questioning him. But George didn't answer because, after all, he didn't know who this person was. And so the man just shot him."

"Well, it wasn't George. Maybe it was someone with the same name but it wasn't George. I'll prove it to you. Come on — right now, all three of us, let's go."

The trailer park was small, the kind that looked as if it had just grown there, a single narrow U curving in from 36th Street and then back out again, doors and windows open, children playing on the road.

Patrik pulled in beside the second unit, a small white trailer that was closed down tight, no sign of life. This must be it. He told Lorraine and the boy to wait.

Patrik walked out onto the road. Farther down he could see a group of young men standing around drinking beer. As he watched one of these separated himself from the others and walked towards Patrik; he was older than the rest, grey eyes, somewhere in his mid-thirties.

"Are you the manager?"

"That's right. What can I do for you?"

"There was a killing here, several weeks ago. I'd like to ... well, I'd like to see where it happened."

"All right." For a moment the manager looked at Patrik. "Come on," he said. "Right over here."

They walked together towards the closed trailer. The manager unlocked the door, climbing in. Patrik followed.

"It's been almost a month now, but I kept it empty. Figured his family might come around."

It was almost dark. Patrik stood just inside the door, the manager a few feet away. No one moved. Finally the manager spoke.

"I'm sorry about it, man. He was a gentle kind of guy." The manager glanced at Patrik, " ... said he was an artist."

Patrik looked away, towards the window.

"Place is cleaned up now," the manager paused, "nothing much here ... some clothes and things in the back."

Patrik held steady. It was impossible to speak; too much was rushing through him, so he just ... maintained.

The manager waited.

"I was hoping," Patrik tried to steady himself, "there was some mistake."

The manager nodded. Again, for several seconds he watched Patrik. "I'd like to show you something," he said finally. "I didn't show it to anyone else." He paused. "You're all right, aren't you?"

"Yeah. I'm okay."

"Come on, then." They left the unit together and began walking across the grass.

"You see, she took him in but, well, she had other friends too. People always coming and going — up all night, that kind of thing."

They had come to another trailer now, hidden back behind some trees. "So I let him have the key to this place," the manager unlocked the door and they went in, "you know, so he could work."

Patrik looked around. In the middle of the small room stood a make-shift easel, a mix of charcoals on the shelf beneath it. It was dusk in Miami now, and the room had a softness to it, an intimacy.

"Look here," the manager moved against the wall. Several canvases were stacked there, turned backwards. He knelt down on one knee and turned over the first. Patrik knelt beside him. My God, it was a rough sketch but there was no mistaking it. It was Coats.

Patrik studied the picture. The next: Taylor. And then another: Smith … Smith and Connors in the bunkhouse playing cards.

"I wouldn't want the wrong person to get hold of these," the manager spoke softly, " … seem kind of personal."

Suddenly Patrik stood. "I need to ask you some questions."

The manager got up slowly. "Sure thing. No problem." He sighed deeply. Then, moving to the open doorway, he stood for a moment looking out across the darkening yard. Lorraine, the boy, and the dog were outside of the car now, standing together, partially visible through the trees.

"That's a beautiful family."

For an instant the room was silent — frozen, like one of the pictures.

"You were born in Miami, weren't you?" The manager moved, lighting a cigarette. The room was dark.

"That's right."

"Been away long?"

"Six years."

"I see." The manager moved inside the room again. "He's being held downtown, the man you want to know about. He didn't try to get away. We would have stopped him if he did. But he didn't. He thought that George was still alive, kept telling everyone to cover him, kept saying George was going to die if someone didn't cover him."

"Has he been charged?"

The manager nodded. "He won't get out. He's just a kid. And now his life is over too."

Patrik looked steadily at the manager. "You're a cop, aren't you — Metro."

The manager nodded. "I was. Not anymore."

"I recognize you."

"I recognize you too." He paused. "We've come full circle, haven't we?"

Patrik didn't answer. For a long time he looked at the man before him. He walked past him then, and stood for a moment in the doorway, looking out.

Lorraine and the boy must have seen him because as he watched they began to approach, hand in hand across the grass.

They make a picture themselves, he was thinking. Of Miami. Where life can be cut down, and hope destroyed. Yet still remain.

Lorraine was close to him now. She took another step. He looked at her — into her eyes. His friend.

He looked down at the boy. His son. And Patrik stepped down onto the grass, and went and took his little family to him. And because this was the most important thing he ever did, he held them very close, and very still. Until they knew.

Historical Note

This is a work of fiction inspired in part by first-hand accounts of the beatings that actually occurred at the Florida Industrial School for Boys during the middle of the last century. The abuses suffered by the children at that school, as well as recent attempts to obtain judicial redress, are well documented. See www.thewhitehouseboys.com.

Although the events in this book are fictional, the horrific beatings, the leather strap with the steel insert and the dungeon-like cold box did exist. The aberrations of the fictional Murdok, the diabolical sessions in which he tortured his victims, although real, have been briefly depicted here in the form of an imagined story not to protect the human monsters whom he represents, but rather to protect their victims. Many of these victims have come forward voluntarily. The reader is encouraged to seek out their stories.

Throughout this novel, locations and place names have been used fictitiously, and incidents and dialogue have been re-invented. And yet, the line between fiction and reality is often blurred. The adventures of our two courageous teens were inspired by the adventures of two real teens. I tell you this because it is the truth of Patrik and George, not any trick or fabrication of the written word, that is recorded here and stands as testament to many lives, lives cut down, destroyed too soon, yet lives — are you listening, George? — that did have meaning, after all.

Most of all, however, this story is an attempt to do justice to the tremendous loyalty and courage, the unbreakable bond that can form between victims of injustice and abuse. Of the hundreds of children who survived unimaginable suffering at the Florida Industrial School for Boys and then went on to carry the cross of these memories throughout their lives, this story is a small but heartfelt tribute.

Acknowledgments

Many thanks to Roger Dean Kiser who first brought to light publicly the atrocities that occurred at the Florida Industrial School for Boys at Marianna, in the middle of the last century, and to the many courageous men who have come forward to verify them, corroborating stories I had once dismissed as much too horrible to be true.

Many thanks to Persia White for her help, her input, and her commitment to this story, to Mecca White for her artistic skill in directing the cover design, to Steve for his humor, his support, and his help with the title, and to James, Laura and Laurie for the faith and love they have always displayed.

And finally, many thanks to my editor, David Collins, for his calm and patient approach, his generous and invaluable advice, and most of all, his constant encouragement.

www.ingramcontent.com/pod-product-compliance
Lightning Source LLC
Chambersburg PA
CBHW060123260626
47160CB00005B/1991

* 9 7 8 1 5 9 5 9 4 3 7 9 8 *